He looked at her for a long moment, then stood up and walked across to where she stood. As he looked down at her Tessa suddenly experienced an odd sinking sensation in the pit of her stomach. He was standing so close that she could smell the faint spiciness of his aftershave mingling with the more antiseptic aroma of the Savlon solution he had used on baby Darren's cut. The silence between them crackled with something she couldn't define and it unnerved her. She took a step backward, putting out her hand blindly for the door handle. Paul registered her uncertainty and felt a small stab of triumph. He might have capitulated professionally—at least for the time being—but he could still exert his masculinity.

'You know,' he said softly, 'it seems to me that we're having the practice meeting Rosemary wanted right here and now. The others might as well have gone home!'

Sarah Franklin lives in Cambridgeshire with her husband, cat and a 'very bossy but lovable' dog. She has always been interested in anything medical. Both her daughters, before marriage, were working in the field of medicine; one as a nurse, the other as an aesthetician, and Sarah herself has been a keen member of the St John Ambulance Brigade and holds their certificates for nursing and first aid. Writing and researching the medical content of her books takes up most of her time, but her hobbies include gardening, the theatre and music as well as 'dabbling with a paint brush'. This is her eighteenth Doctor Nurse Romance. Other titles include *A Surgeon's Sacrifice, Crisis!* and *A Routine Appointment.*

MIRACLES TAKE LONGER

BY

SARAH FRANKLIN

MILLS & BOON LIMITED
ETON HOUSE   18-24 PARADISE ROAD
RICHMOND   SURREY   TW9 1SR

First published in Great Britain 1988
by Mills & Boon Limited

© Sarah Franklin 1988

Australian copyright 1988
Philippine copyright 1988
This edition 1988

ISBN 0 263 76276 9

Set in Plantin 10 on 11 pt.
03 8812 58459

Typeset in Great Britain by JCL Graphics, Bristol

Made and Printed in Great Britain.

CHAPTER ONE

'LOOK, MUMMY—houses! Are we nearly there?' Six-year-old Beverley, her face pressed eagerly to the train window, asked the question for the hundredth time since they had left Manchester early that morning. Tessa shifted her eyes from the book on her lap to the sprawling mass of small red brick houses flashing past. She glanced at her watch and saw that it was almost three, then as she looked up again she caught sight of the towering bulk of Oakmoor Cathedral rising majestically on its hill in the distance, its turreted towers gleaming in the sunlight.

'Yes, darling, I believe we *are* nearly there,' she said, leaning forward with her small daughter to watch the changing landscape. A small spiral of nervous excitement began somewhere in the pit of her stomach. As they drew closer to the city of Oakmoor it seemed to her that her future came inexorably closer. This was the beginning of a new life for Tessa and her small daughter; a fresh start that carried with it a challenge. She hoped with all her heart she was strong enough to make a success of it. The prospect excited and terrified her both at the same time.

Feeling a sudden need for comfort and reassurance, she pulled Beverley on to her knee and began to point out the landmarks that she herself had seen only once before, when she had come to Oakmoor for her interview at the Laughton Mere Health Centre three weeks before.

'Look, that's the Cathedral,' she said. 'It was built a very long time ago—almost six hundred years. At night they light it all up and you can see it for miles around, shining just like a fairytale castle; like Camelot in the story,

5

remember?'

Beverley's bright intelligent little face lit up with anticipation. 'Will you take me to see it? Is this a really *big* city like London, Mummy? Is there a zoo—and a skating rink?'

Tessa ruffled the silky dark curls and laughed. 'Maybe. We'll have to see, shan't we? I shouldn't be surprised, though. You know, Oakmoor was just a small city not so long ago, but it's grown and grown over the last few years so that it has lots of things now that it never used to have.'

'Why has it grown?' Beverley wanted to know, looking at Tessa enquiringly with huge dark eyes.

'Well, the big cities like London were getting very crowded, so the people started to move here where the air is cleaner and there's more space.' Tessa had always believed in explaining things to her daughter as fully as the child was able to understand. 'There are lots of new factories here for the people to work in and lots of new houses where they can live—like those——' she pointed to the large estate spread out almost as far as the eye could see from the train.

'And schools? They do have schools, don't they?' Beverley asked eagerly.

Tessa laughed. 'Yes, love, they do have schools. Lovely new ones, with lots of nice new friends for you to make.'

Beverley's big brown eyes regarded her mother's face seriously for a moment. 'Shall we like it here, Mummy?'

'Yes, darling,' Tessa nodded positively.

'And will Granny come and see us sometimes?'

'Of course, when we get settled in a place of our own.'

Beverley sighed. 'I hope Granny will be all right without us. I shall miss her, won't you?'

Inwardly Tessa echoed her daughter's sigh. She would certainly miss her mother—much more than she would have cared to admit; for the help and support she had come to rely on so much as well as for her company. Ever since

Beverley had been born Tessa's mother had been there—a tower of strength, doing her best to fill the gap left by the father Beverley had never known. Without her it would have been quite impossible for Tessa to have qualified—first as a nurse, later as a family therapist. But increasingly over the past year Tessa had noticed the strain in the older woman's eyes, seen the weariness she had tried so hard to hide, and realised for the first time that for all her outward strength, her mother wasn't getting any younger. It was high time she had a life of her own and a little of the leisure she deserved. Tessa had come to the conclusion that the time had come for her and Beverley to stand as a family on their own, and the more she thought about it, the more she knew she was right. When she had been offered this job she had grasped the opportunity with both hands, sure, in spite of her mother's protests, that she was doing the right thing for all three of them. But that did nothing to dispel the secret scared feeling that churned her stomach each time she thought about the future; the same feeling of apprehension she felt now as she hugged her small daughter to her and stared out at the speeding landscape.

As the rain slid into Oakmoor Central Station and drew to a halt there was a scramble to collect their luggage together and alight. Tessa had sent as much as she could on in advance, but they still had two large cases and a holdall with the odds and ends they had needed for the journey. A kindly man helped Tessa with the larger of the two cases and lifted Beverley out on to the platform, where they stood hand in hand amid the jostling mass of people, Tessa's eyes searching the sea of faces for one familiar one she was sure would be there.

Sure enough, Dr Rosemary Denning stood waiting by the barrier. The train was dead on time and she had arrived at the station just as it was pulling in. She breathed a sigh of relief. She had been determined to be waiting when Tessa arrived.

It had been sheer chance, meeting Tessa again at the one-day course six weeks ago where she had been lecturing. A lucky chance, she told herself. They had first met at St Luke's Hospital in the East End of London, where Tessa had trained and later worked as staff nurse on the maternity wing. At that time Rosemary—a newly qualified young doctor herself—had been attached to the firm of Mark Gillings, the obstetrician. She had witnessed Tessa's whirlwind romance with a former patient and watched helplessly as it progressed into a disastrous marriage. From the first she had seen all the danger signs yet had had to standy by, powerless to help or advise two young people who were too much in love to be able to see how wrong they were for each other.

Rosemary had always felt that Tessa was a great loss to the profession, but she had understood the pressure she had felt as a single parent struggling to bring up her small daughter. As Beverley grew from baby to active toddler she obviously wanted to spend more time with her and to take some of the pressure off her mother.

They'd had a lot of news to catch up on that day at the course, over a shared lunch, and it was when Rosemary had learned of Tessa's new qualification as a family therapist that the idea she had been playing with for months had begun to look like an exciting reality instead of just a pipe-dream.

Settled now with her husband, Dr John Denning, as joint senior partners at Laughton Mere Health Centre on the outskirts of the growing overspill city of Oakmoor, she had long dreamed of being able to offer more than medical advice to the wide cross-section of the public that made up their patients. Tessa had just the kind of nursing experience required, and now she had this invaluable added qualification too. She had outlined her plan for forming a family counselling group to Tessa that day and found the girl enthusiastic and full of ideas. By the time she arrived home at Oakmoor that evening she had it all clearly worked out in her mind.

John, her husband, had been guardedly optimistic at first, and so had Dr James Lamb, their associate. The seemingly unfounded doubts of Paul Nathan, the junior partner in the practice, didn't worry Rosemary unduly. She was convinced that if she couldn't convince him of the advantages of the scheme, Tessa soon would. Their present practice nurse was about to leave, so there would be a formal vacancy to offer Tessa. They could take it from there. She had persuaded them to agree to meet Tessa, ringing her later that week to invite her to Oakmoor for the weekend to see round the place and have an informal interview with John, James and herself. After that the plan had rapidly gathered momentum, and within a few weeks the details had been finalised and Rosemary had written to offer Tessa the job.

Searching the teeming mass of faces, Rosemary caught a glimpse of a tall dark girl holding a small child by the hand. Tessa! And that must be little Beverley. She would never have recognised the child. Last time she had seen her she had been in a pram! She waved frantically, standing on tiptoe to be seen above the bobbing heads.

'Tessa! Hey, Tessa—over here!'

Tessa's face broke into a smile of relief as she picked up the cases. 'There she is, Beverley—there's Auntie Rose. Come on, darling,' she urged her small daughter as she struggled towards the barrier.

Rosemary hugged them both, exclaiming at how tall Beverley had grown. Then, taking one of the cases from Tessa, she led the way to where her car was parked in the station yard.

As they drove Beverley gazed out of the car window in wide-eyed wonderment. It was all so different from the Lancashire village where she had grown up. Much of the town was pedestrianised. In its centre the brand new shopping centre with its adjacent multi-storied car park rose, a mass of glass and concrete, in stark contrast to the mellow stone of the Cathedral standing sentinel on the hill above the town.

They drove westwards out of the valley that held the town. Smaller shops gave way to a large industrial estate, then, as they climbed higher, to houses—masses of them, arranged in small communities where the planners had tried their best to avoid the monotonous serried rows of years gone by, arranging them round little squares planted with shrubs and trees. There were attractive shopping centres, large open play areas, schools and community centres.

'They seem to have thought of everything,' Tessa remarked as they made their way on to Laughton Mere.

Rosemary shook her head. 'Everything except the diversity of human nature,' she remarked wryly. 'Throw all classes, cultures and races together and you have a recipe for problems with a capital P, I'm afraid.'

The Dennings lived in one of the original villages still sitting incongruously amid the new developments; a reminder of a bygone age with its quaint church and drowsing thatched cottages. Beverley's face brightened. This place looked more like home. Birch House stood close to the village green, a pretty L-shaped stone house surrounded by a rambling old-fashioned garden and enclosed by a tall yew hedge.

As they drove into the garage Rosemary spoke to them over her shoulder as she unlatched her seat belt. 'You'll be our guests for the weekend, naturally. Tomorrow I'll take you to meet Nell Orton, Tessa. She can offer you and

Beverley a couple of rooms if you want them. She's a freelance journalist and works at home, so if the pair of you hit it off it could work ideally for you. She had two children of her own at school in Laughton and she'd be willing to meet Beverley for you when your hours didn't work in.'

Tessa felt Beverley's small hand creep apprehensively into hers, and she gave it a squeeze, glancing down at her daughter. 'Oh—well, thank you, Rose, but I wouldn't want to impose——' she began hesitantly.

Rosemary laughed. 'Impose! You haven't met Nell. She loves kids. She'd fill the house with them if she could.' She grinned at Beverley. 'And I know she's going to spoil you to bits! Her own children are too big to cuddle now and she's really looking forward to some serious mothering again.' She helped Beverley out of the car. 'Oh, by the way, she's a single parent, like you.'

She hauled Tessa's suitcase out of the boot. 'Come on, you two. My Mrs Grange has been making jelly and butterfly cakes all afternoon in honour of this young lady.' She took Beverley's hand. 'Later I'll take you both for a walk round the village. I've arranged a little dinner party for this evening, Tessa, so that you can meet your new colleagues.'

The kitchen at Birch House was the old-fashioned kind, with a pine dreser and an Aga in front of which snoozed two enormous tabby cats. Mrs Grange sat Beverley at the big table in the centre of the room and placed before her a tempting array of all the things she knew children liked, while Rosemary and Tessa drank tea and caught up with their news. Though no one said anything, all three women noticed with some dismay that Beverley hardly touched a thing.

As Tessa put her daughter to bed that evening in the large double bed in the Dennings' guest room, the little girl reached up to wind her arms around her mother's neck.

'I like it here, Mummy,' she whispered. 'Can't we stay here instead of going to that other lady's house?'

Tessa sat on the edge of the bed. 'We can't stay here, darling,' she said gently. 'This is Auntie Rose and Uncle John's home. Maybe later we'll get a house of our own, but until we've saved enough money for that we have to make a home where we can.'

Beverley's face crumpled. 'I want *you* to meet me from school,' she said in a small voice. 'Or Granny, like before. I don't want this Nell lady to meet me. I don't want to live with her either.'

Tessa took one of the small hands in hers and squeezed it. She knew how bewildered and insecure Beverley must be feeling, she didn't feel much happier about the arrangement herself, but beggars couldn't be choosers.

'You haven't met her yet, darling,' she said gently. 'I'm sure she's very nice. And she has two children of her own, so there'll be someone for you to play with right there in the same house. You've never had that before, now have you?'

Beverley shook her head. 'N-oo—but I'd rather have Granny.' She looked at Tessa, her brown eyes pleading as she whispered: 'Mummy, couldn't we go home—*please*?'

Tessa didn't believe in hedging, or making promises she knew she couldn't keep. Beverley must learn to face up to the truth, and the sooner the better. She bent forward to smooth the dark curls back from the child's brow. 'Granny is very tired, darling,' she said. 'She looked after us for a very long time and it was hard work. We don't want her to get ill, do we? You're a big girl now and the time has come when you and I must take care of each other.' She kissed the soft little cheek. 'We both have to learn to be strong and help each other. I need you to try very hard for me. I know you'll do your best, won't you?'

Beverley answered the question with a tremulous smile.

'All right, Mummy, I'll try,' she said bravely.

As Tessa regarded her daughter a little of the old anger rose in her heart; anger against the man she had once loved so passionately—the man who was Beverley's father and who had deserted them both so heartlessly when they had needed him most. She stood up abruptly, squaring her shoulders, determined not to dwell on the bitterness of the past. She and Beverley were fine. They could manage, she told herself firmly. Just as long as they had each other. That was the important thing.

Bending she tucked the bedclothes protectively around the small curled body. 'Go to sleep now, sweetheart,' she whispered. 'Everything will look better in the morning. We're going to have a brand new life here—all sorts of exciting adventures. Just you wait and see!'

Rosemary was waiting when Tessa came downstairs, a glass of sherry ready poured. She held out her hand welcomingly.

'Come and sit down. I'm sure you're tired after the journey and settling in. Has Beverley gone off all right?'

Tessa nodded. 'She's feeling a bit strange and more than a little homesick, but she'll be fine.'

Rosemary nodded sympathetically. 'Poor little scrap, it must be very disturbing for her. But children are resilient little things. She'll soon shake down.' She took a sip of her sherry, regarding her friend appreciatively. Tessa had changed into a pretty flowered dress of cool jade green and white and applied fresh make-up. With her hair in the smooth brown shoulder-length bob she still looked absurdly young. Her serene face belied the trauma she had suffered over the breakdown of her brief marriage. Only the firm chin and the proud tilt of her head hinted at the determined character wrought in her by past events.

'You're looking very nice, Tessa. More relaxed than the last time I saw you.' Rosemary looked at her watch. 'John'll be here as soon as surgery's over, any minute now. James Lamb, whom you've already met, is coming too.' She cleared her throat. 'And I've invited Dr Paul Nathan, our junior partner. He was away when you came for your interview, so you haven't met him. I—er thought you should get to know each other—at least, meet before you begin work at the Centre on Monday.'

Tessa glanced at Rosemary, sensing a certain awkwardness in her tone. 'Is anything wrong?' she asked. 'Is there something I should know before I meet Dr Nathan?'

'Good heavens, no!' Rosemary laughed—a little too lightly, Tessa thought. Rosemary met her direct gaze and the smile melted from her face. 'Oh dear, I should have known there was no beating about the bush with you. I may was well tell you, I suppose. The truth of it is that Paul's not completely in favour of my ideas for the family therapy group. Not that it makes any difference,' she added hurriedly. 'He's the only one with reservations. We shall just have to convince him, and I'm sure that with your help we'll have no difficulties there.'

'What are his objections?' Tessa asked, her heart sinking. She hadn't bargained for opposition.

Rosemary shrugged. 'He thinks it smacks of interference. He says people should be left alone to sort out their own problems—stand on their own feet.'

'That's all very well for the strong, but what if they're not able to?'

Rosemary shook her head. 'Paul is a very independent person,' she explained. 'Very strong and stoic. Not only does he "not suffer fools gladly", as they say, but he hasn't much understanding for the weak either.'

Tessa pulled a face. 'He doesn't sound very sympathetic. I'm not sure I like the sound of Dr Nathan.'

'Oh, he's an excellent doctor,' Rosemary assured her

hurriedly. 'He isn't unkind or unsympathetic, don't think that. His particular hobby-horse is preventive medicine. He's a very clever—and a very nice man.' Rosemary could see that Tessa wasn't convinced. Maybe she had gone over the top—should she have left her to make up her own mind She tried a different angle: 'I think it all stems from his background,' she said. 'He's the product of one of those spartan public schools—all cold showers and violent exercise. Then since he's been here a rather and unfortunate situation has developed. The last practice nurse . . .' She broke off with obvious relief as the front door slammed, heralding the arrival of her husband, John, accompanied by his partner. Dr James Lamb was a tall, grey-haired man in his early fifties whom Tessa had met at her interview and found pleasant and friendly.

Both men greeted her warmly, asking politely after her daughter and enquiring whether they had had a good journey.

Looking round, Rosemary asked her husband where Paul was, and he replied that he was parking his car.

Tessa was standing with her back to the door, talking to John a few minutes later, when he looked over her shoulder and said: 'Ah, Paul. I'd like you to meet our new practice nurse and family therapist, Tessa Trentham. Tessa, this is Dr Paul Nathan.'

She turned to find herself looking up into a pair of cool blue eyes. They were a curiously bright blue, almost luminous, and her first impression of the icy gleam in them was hardly encouraging. He was considerably taller than she, at least six foot, and the aquiline nose he looked down at her seemed to intensify his disdainful expression. She took in the rather angular features; the wide mouth—incapable of compromise, she told herself. Only the square chin with its marked cleft showed any hope that he was capable of humour. He inclined his head and the corners of his mouth lifted in a smile that left the eyes unchanged.

'How do you do?'

'I'm well, thank you.' She offered her hand. 'And you?'

He nodded. 'Fine.' The hand that took hers was like his eyes—cool and hard. It touched her fingers only briefly, releasing them as though he found the contact unpleasant. Tessa decided there and then that it wasn't going to be easy to like Dr Paul Nathan.

Over dinner Rosemary purposely kept the conversation light, not touching on work at all. As she told Tessa in the kitchen later when they went to make coffee: 'This evening is purely for the purpose of getting to know each other. I want it to be a relaxed occasion.'

Privately, Tessa guessed that her friend was intent on avoiding a discussion that might possibly develop into an argument. But it was inevitable that before the evening was over a controversial subject should arise, and it was as they sat over coffee in the Dennings' lounge later that the subject suddenly swung on to one-parent families.

'We seem to have rather more than our fair share of them here in Laughton Mere,' Paul remarked. 'All crying out for Government assistance as though it was their birthright. It will never cease to be a mystery to me in this enlightened day and age why there are so many.'

Tessa felt herself stiffen. 'Surely there are any number of reasons,' she said quietly. 'There have never been as many pressures on family life as there are today. Once people were content with their lot, but today the media show so many other facets of life, much of which are totally unrelated to real life. People tend to expect too much—and when disappointment sets in . . .'

He stared at her as though she were talking gibberish. 'Yes, I've heard that argument. Certainly they expect too much! Personally I don't believe in the fashionable trend for making excuses. You have to admit that they're a drain on resources, whatever the reason for their state. I'd say that in nine out of ten cases it's just plain irresponsibility.'

'Isn't that rather a sweeping statement?' Tessa's heartbeat quickened as his words struck a spark of stinging resentment within her. She heard her tone harden and felt her face beginning to burn. Out of the corner of her eye she could see Rosemary sending mute distress signals to her husband.

John began to speak, but at that moment the door opened and a small figure in Snoopy pyjamas stood on the threshold.

'Mummy, I can't find Teddy.' Beverley rubbed her eyes, blinking at the light. 'I woke up and he wasn't there.'

Tessa jumped up. 'I'll find him, darling. I think he's still in the case.' At the door she turned. 'Excuse me, will you? I won't be long.'

As the door closed behind her Paul Nathan grimaced and blew out his breath. 'Damn! Why didn't somebody tell me?'

Rosemary stared at him. 'I think you know my views on labelling people, Paul,' she said pointedly. 'You were prejudiced enough as it was.'

John cleared his throat. 'Shall we change the subject? More coffee, anyone?' He stood up and lifted the coffee pot, looking round hopefully at his guests.

Paul looked at his watch and stood up. 'Not for me. I have a patient I'm not too happy about. I'd like to look in on him before I turn in. Thanks for the dinner, Rose. Goodnight, everyone.' At the door he turned. 'Oh, by the way, make my apologies for me, will you?'

As the door closed behind him Rosemary pulled a face. '*Chicken!*' she muttered scathingly.

CHAPTER TWO

NELL ORTON lived in what had once been St Mary's Vicarage. It was a large rambling Victorian house, and Rosemary told Tessa that it had replaced a beautiful Georgian one that had been pulled down in 1860 to make way for it.

'No preservation orders in those days,' she remarked. 'But they weren't allowed to demolish this one when they built the new modern vicarage at the other end of the village, which is how this white elephant still happens to be standing.'

They stood at the gate, looking up at the twin neo-Gothic gables and imposing entrance porch with its stained-glass panels and coloured tiles.

'In those days parsons were renowned for their large families,' Rosemary said with a smile. 'Nell has five bedrooms and she likes to supplement her income by letting a couple of them out—usually to students or people who really need somewhere homely and cheap.'

Tessa had already heard a little about Nell Orton from Rosemary on their walk across the village green. She knew, for instance, that she too was divorced and that she had two children, a boy and a girl, who lived with her and attended local schools. Rosemary had already said that Nell loved children and was looking forward to having a small child in the house again, and sure enough, when she answered the door it was Beverley she greeted first.

'Hello, you must be Beverley. Come along in, love.' She bent down and held out welcoming arms. The look of apprehension melted from Beverley's face as she responded instinctively.

Nell was tall and well built. She wore a loose-fitting Indian print dress and her long brown hair hung in a thick plait over her left shoulder. Her open, rosy face was devoid of make-up, but her skin gleamed with health and the clear hazel eyes shone with vitality. She ushered them into her living room, which clearly doubled as a study. Apologising for the clutter, she swept papers from the table and hurriedly threw a cover over her typewriter.

'I've been trying to finish an article,' she explained. 'The deadline was Friday.' She grinned. 'Thank goodness I can quite feasibly blame the post!' She shooed a large black cat off the settee. 'Do sit down. I'll make some coffee.' She bent to smile into Beverley's face. 'And I've got some homemade lemondade for you—and I bet you like chocolate bikkies too, eh?'

Beverley beamed, nodding. 'Yes, please.'

'Good. There's a big garden out at the back, with a swing,' Nell told her. 'It's madly overgrown, but the kids like playing jungles out there. There's a tree-house too,' she added. 'One of the students who stayed here last year made it.' She ruffled Beverley's curly hair. 'Oh, yes, you're going to love it here. And I'm going to love having you too!'

Tessa relaxed, warming to Nell's informal, free and easy manner. She seemed to have taken it for granted that they'd be staying, and suddenly Tessa wondered why she had ever doubted that she would.

When they had finished their coffee Nell took Beverley into the garden and introduced her to her own two children, Ben and Zoe. Each of them took one of Beverley's hands and led her off on a tour of the rambling garden. Nell smiled at Tessa as she watched them go.

'Nothing to worry about there. She's going to fit in a treat. My two'll be in their element with a new chick to take under their wings. They take after me, for their sins!'

She walked back towards the house. 'Come on in and I'll show you the rooms.'

On the landing she said: 'I thought you could make one of them into a sitting room if you liked. Somewhere to retreat to when we get too much for you! I warn you, we can be an exhausting lot.' Her laugh rang out gaily. Tessa and Rosemary looked at each other and smiled. The relaxed feel of the Orton household appealed to them both.

It was arranged that Tessa and Beverley move into the two first-floor rooms immediately. They overlooked the overgrown garden where a riot of rambling roses and hollyhocks mingled happily with dandelions and daisies. They were comfortably if shabbily furnished, and Nell suggested that they could be rearranged to make a sitting room and a bedroom with the minimum of trouble.

'You may want to have somewhere to entertain,' she said. 'I'd like you to feel free to come and go as you please. We don't stand on ceremony here.'

Back in the living room they arranged terms, and Nell remarked that she would be happy to collect Beverley from school when Tessa was working. 'The best thing about my job is that I'm always here,' she said. 'And there are no rules. Everyone just mucks in.'

They had the greatest difficulty in dragging Beverley away from her new friends, and it was only when Tessa had promised that they would be moving in later that day that she agreed reluctantly to leave.

After lunch they left Beverley with John while Rosemary took Tessa on a tour of the Health Centre. They entered the new part of the village by way of a little bridge over a stream that fed the mere from which the village had derived its name, and at once Tessa was struck by the contrast between the picturesque thatched cottages of the old village and the raw brick-built terraces built around the little squares.

The Health Centre was newly built and stood on the edge of the shopping mall, surrounded by its own spacious car park. The Centre housed an infant welfare clinic, chiropody and dental surgeries as well as the surgeries of the four doctors. Rosemary showed Tessa the well equipped room that she would occupy as practice nurse.

'I thought we might introduce the family therapy group by having a meeting one Saturday afternoon,' she said. 'We could have it in the Community Centre next door, there are plenty of meeting rooms. I thought we could lay on tea and sandwiches for the introductory session—make it a bit of an occasion so as to break the ice.'

'How will you advertise it?' Tessa asked.

'Well, I thought posters—here at the Health Centre and in the Community Centre too. Then there are the newsagent's and chemist's—places like that,' Rosemary told her. 'In a community like this word soon gets round.' She grinned. 'And a free tea might tip the balance where the more cautious are concerned! You'd introduce yourself and give a little explanatory talk,' she went on. 'I've asked a friend who's a child psychologist to come and speak, and a social worker I know is willing to give up a Saturday afternoon for us too.'

'Sounds good,' Tessa said, trying not to show her apprehension at the thought of standing up and addressing a roomful of strangers. 'And after that?'

'A weekly group session where people could share problems and pool their experience,' Rosemary said. 'Presided over by you, of course. Then I thought you might have a regular surgery of your own, if the demand arises, where people who wanted private help might come and get your advice in confidence.'

'Sounds great,' Tessa said, feeling a tingle of anticipation at the interesting new job she saw opening up before her.

Rosmeary spread her hands. 'Look, there are a couple of

things that need attention in my room before I go home.
Why don't you have a good look round in here—familiarise
yourself with the place. Alison Moss, our last practice
nurse, was very methodical, so I think you'll find
everything in apple-pie order, but I daresay there are things
you'll want to arrange differently. You'll find your
uniforms in the cupboard, by the way. I think they'll fit,
but you'll want to check on that too.'

When she had gone Tessa looked round, opening
cupboards and drawers to familiarise herself with the
whereabouts of the things she would need. But having
checked that there were plenty of spare supplies she found
there was nothing she wanted to change. She sat down at
the desk, imagining herself working here. It felt good. In
the past year, since her training as a family therapist had
been completed, she had not worked in a full-time job at all.
To take the burden off her mother's shoulders she had
worked as an agency nurse and done a good deal of night
duty at the local hospital, which gave her most of the
daytime hours free. It had been as tiring as a full-time job
and not nearly as fulfilling, and she had had no chance to
try out her new skills at all.

In the full-length cupboard Rosemary had indicated
behind the desk she found three blue uniform dresses and a
boxful of white caps, with a plentiful supply of disposable
aprons and gloves. She took one of the dresses out and held
it against herself, trying it for size. It seemed about right,
but she decided she'd better try one on to make sure.
Slipping out of her skirt and blouse, she pulled the dress
over her head and buttoned it, smoothing down the skirt
and turning to look at herself in the mirror. Yes, with her
own belt with its SRN buckle around the waist it should be
fine, she told herself. But at that moment she was startled as
through the mirror she saw the door open to admit Dr Paul
Nathan.

She spun round and for a moment they stared at each other, each of them equally startled. Paul was the first to recover.

'I'm sorry, I didn't know anyone was in here.'

Tessa felt her face colouring as though she'd been caught out doing something she shouldn't. 'It's quite all right. Rosemary brought me to look round and I-I thought I'd better try on my uniform in case . . .' The stumbling words trailed off. She was furious with herself, both for feeling she had to explain her presence and for blushing and stumbling as she did so. After all, she had more right to be in the room than *he* had. A moment sooner and he would have walked in on her in her bra and pants! The thought made her blush an even deeper pink. 'Did you want something?' she asked a trifle stiffly.

'I seem to have run out of disposable syringes,' he said. 'I was looking for something else and I noticed. I wondered if Alison—if there were any in here.' To her extreme annoyance he went to the desk and began searching the drawers for them.

Tessa crossed to the cupboard where she had seen them stored and took out an unopened box. 'Are these what you're looking for?' she asked. 'There seem to be plenty.' She held out the box, her brown eyes meeting his cool blue ones candidly. 'And if you run out of anything again you only have to ask.'

It was immediately clear that the slight emphasis she placed on the word *ask* had not escaped his notice. 'Thanks—I will.' He regarded her for a long moment. 'You seem to have made yourself very much at home,' he remarked coolly.

Her chin lifted. 'That was the idea.'

'Naturally.' He nodded as though conceding the point and walked towards the door. Reaching it, he turned and cleared his throat. 'I-believe I owe you an apology.'

'Really? For what?' Tessa asked.

'For the things I said last night. I didn't know your circumstances, you see. No one saw fit to warn me.'

'That's all right. Everyone has a perfect right to their opinions anyway,' Tessa returned. 'As for no one *warning* you, there's really no reason why they should. After all, I have a daughter, not an infectious disease. And incidentally, I don't see her as some kind of handicap.'

A flicker of irritation crossed his face. 'Then may I ask why you're so touchy on the subject?' He frowned and held up his hand. 'No! I'm sorry. Forget I said that.' He gave her a wry smile. 'That's the second apology I've made in as many minutes! It isn't a habit of mine, I assure you. Look, as we're going to work together I really think we should try to be on good terms.' He looked enquiringly at her.

Tessa nodded, swallowing her resentment. 'I agree, naturally.'

He hesitated for a moment as though struggling to make up his mind, then he walked back across the room to perch on the corner of her desk, his arms folded as he regarded her gravely. 'Perhaps the best way to be on good terms is to be frank with each other,' he said. 'I think it's only fair to tell you that I'm not entirely in favour of this group therapy thing Rose is so keen on. But as I was outvoted on the matter . . .'

'You don't have to be involved if you don't agree,' Tessa interrupted. 'So it needn't cause you any extra work.'

'My reason for objecting goes rather deeper than that!' he said vehemently. 'And as some of the people you'll be dealing with will inevitably be my patients I can hardly avoid being involved.'

'In which case you'll be able to report back on the improvements you find,' Tessa countered.

Paul Nathan grunted noncommittally and rose to his feet, turning again towards the door. 'I only wish I could share your optimism and obvious enthusiasm, Miss Trentham.'

Tessa felt her colour rise again. 'Actually, it's Mrs,' she told him. It seemed he had judged her already. Did he make the same snap decisions about everyone he met? she wondered.

'I'm sorry—*Mrs* Trentham.' He stared back at her unrepentantly. 'If you want my opinion—which of course I realise you *don't!*—there are certain people who'll make a mess of their lives whatever anyone does. They head for disaster from the moment of birth—like lemmings.' He shrugged. 'But good luck anyway.'

'Thank you.' She bristled with indignation. Obviously he had intended the barbed remark for her. It was totally uncalled for and very unkind. 'Thank you *so* much, Dr Nathan,' she said, unable to keep the sarcasm out of her voice. 'How very kind of you!'

Tessa was still trembling when she went in search of Rosemary a few minutes after Paul had left, but she didn't recount their conversation to her; merely mentioning that Paul had looked in in search of syringes.

'I saw him too,' Rosemary said. 'I knew what had happened the moment I saw his face. He lost a patient with a severe coronary in the early hours. That's why he was here—writing up the report.'

'Oh!' Tessa was taken aback. 'I'm sorry to hear that. He didn't say.'

Rosemary shook her head. 'He wouldn't. It takes us all in different ways. John always goes quiet and thoughtful, but when it happens to Paul it seems to make him angry; almost as though he takes it as a personal affront.'

'He wished me luck with the job,' Tessa said, almost to herself.

'Rosemary's eyebrows shot up. 'Well! That was generous considering his views on family therapy. You must have made a hit!'

Tessa sighed. 'I hardly think so, somehow.'

When Tessa and Beverley arrived at the Old Vicarage that evening Nell had already moved the furniture. One room housed the two beds while the other was furnished with a table and chairs, a settee and two comfortable chairs.

'You really shouldn't have done all this by yourself,' Tessa said, looking round appreciatively.

Nell laughed. 'No trouble. I'm as strong as an ox and I'm well used to humping furniture about. Is it all right for you?'

'It's fine,' Tessa told her, looking round.

Nell smiled and laid a hand on her shoulder. 'Help yourself to the kitchen. It's all yours,' she said. 'I'm not one of those housewives who guards her kitchen jealously like some sacred shrine. In fact there are times when I positively hate it! Come down when you've got Beverley to bed and have a natter and a glass of wine if you feel like it. My door is always open.' She went downstairs, leaving Tessa to unpack and settle in.

As she got Beverley ready for bed the little girl chatted incessantly about Ben and Zoe, her two new friends, and as Tessa bent to kiss her goodnight her daughter looked up at her with wide brown eyes. 'I *like* it here,' she said, happily hugging her teddy bear. 'You were right, Mummy, we're going to have lots of adventures. I think I'm going to like our new life.'

Tessa smiled and heaved a sigh of relief. Well, that was one problem off her mind at least. She only wished that certain other people could be as easily won over.

CHAPTER THREE

DR PAUL NATHAN drove home to his bachelor flat very carefully that Sunday afternoon. He had been up for most of the night before and he knew all too well what lack of sleep could do to his concentration—not to mention his patience.

He had finished writing up his report with a very heavy heart. George Parsons had been his patient for three years; ever since he had joined the practice at Laughton Mere. Since taking early retirement from an exacting job in advertising George had suffered two heart attacks, last night's massive coronary proving fatal.

'The result of too many expense account lunches, long hours and overwork,' Paul repeated to himself. 'Striving for a better standard of life with all the wrong habits.' He shook his head in exasperation. If only more doctors believed as he did in practising preventive medicine instead of handing out tranquillisers and antacids that merely masked the danger signals! it was a depressingly familiar story. George Parsons had been a good, hard-working husband and father. He should have been able to look forward to at least twenty years of happy retirement. Instead he'd left behind a shocked widow and a teenage son at university. 'What a waste,' Paul said aloud as he drew up at the traffic lights. 'What a damned *waste*!'

His thoughts were especially concentrated on George's nineteen-year-old son who had started his first term at university only the previous autumn. Paul was remembering how he had felt when he lost his own father. He had been much younger than David Parsons—just

27

twelve and away at boarding school, which made him feel isolated and helpless. Tragically, his mother had followed just eighteen months later, totally devastating him, though the spartan training he had received since the age of eight had prevented him from allowing his grief to show.

Paul's parents had been older than George Parsons. Marrying late in life, his father had been sixty when Paul was born, his mother in her late forties. Anxious that he should grow up independent and able to stand on his own feet, they had chosen what they thought the best preparation for life, sending him away to boarding school at an early age—something for which Paul had never quite forgiven them, for although he had felt their loss deeply, in actual fact he had never really had time to get to know them.

Driving into the garage, he unfolded his long legs from the car, locked it securely and made his way up the stairs to the flat. Suddenly, for no apparent reason, he recalled his earlier encounter with Tessa Trentham. When Rosemary Denning had unfolded her plans for this new family therapy group to him a few weeks ago, explaining that she had invited an old friend from her hospital days to come for an interview, he had shied away from meeting the woman, making sure to be away that weekend. Secretly he had hoped the whole idea would blow over, but he had returned to find that everything had been cut and dried in his absence. He couldn't deny that he was piqued by the decision, taken without the benefit of his opinion, though of course, as the most junior doctor in the practice, he could hardly complain, especially when he had made his inflexible opinion abundantly clear.

The idea of counselling people who had already made an irresponsible decision to have children—sometimes even without the benefits of marriage—was abhorrent to him. It seemed to him a futile waste of time. Personally he had always been obliged to stand on his own feet—had experienced all too painfully the folly of relying on others. As a child he had naïvely imagined his parents would always be there, but they had died before he had reached his teens. Later, when he was in his teens, the elderly aunt who had taken on his upbringing had become an invalid, forcibly bringing home to him the cruelty of fate and the sheer frailty of human life. He had decided at a very early age that it was best not to count on anything. To be totally self-reliant was the only sure way to emerge whole from life's battles. He was convinced that his plan to steer a solitary course through life was a sound one. And although as a doctor he tried hard to be tolerant, deep inside he had a deeply ingrained aversion to character weakness.

As he prepared his solitary evening meal his thoughts drifted again to the tall, slim, dark-eyed girl who was to be the new practice nurse. After Alison, with her ash-blonde curls and adoring blue eyes, Paul freely admitted that he had hoped the new one would be a motherly middle-aged matron. Tessa did not match this description. In his mind's eye he saw again the candid brown eyes and the defiant tilt of her chin as she had countered his remarks. Damn it, she had been downright impertinent, implying that he should *ask* next time he wanted anything! She hadn't even begun work at the Health Centre yet, and already she was trying to put him in his place! Yet he couldn't prevent a smile from quirking the corners of his mouth as he remembered the warm colour that had flooded her cheeks as she said it. Her cheek was certainly preferable to Alison's tremulous, subservient manner. One careless word and the girl had been on the edge of tears. She had made him feel guilty simply because he found himself unable to return her obvious devotion. And eventually the silent reproach that had emanated from her had very nearly pushed him into looking for another post. The situation had almost reached crisis point when, to his relief, Alison had suddenly announced that she had been offered a job in Kuwait and had decided to accept it.

As Paul Nathan was eating the evening meal, prepared in his immaculate model kitchen, Tessa was chatting to Nell in the cosy, cluttered living room at the Old Vicarage. Sitting on the chintz-covered settee, her feet tucked under her, she relaxed as she sipped the glass of wine Nell poured for her.

'This is delicious,' she remarked. 'What kind is it?'

'Home-made elderberry,' Nell told her with a smile. 'It's my one culinary talent.' She raised her own glass of ruby liquid to the light, viewing it appreciatively. 'It's rather good, if I do say it myself. I'm quite noted for my wine in the village. I once got the entire Mothers' Union tiddly on it. The Vicar has never forgiven me!' She took a sip from her glass as Tessa giggled.

'What happened?' she asked.

'They asked me to donate something to drink at their annual bash and apparently they thought it was fruit cup,' Nell told her. Her eyes sparkled wickedly. 'You'd have been intrigued at some of the inhibitions that were released that evening!' She took another sip. 'Jim Lamb is rather partial to a glass of this when he comes to supper.'

Tessa looked up. 'Do you mean Dr Lamb?' she asked.

'That's right. We're old friends. Jim's wife died five years ago, just before he came to Laughton Mere. He doesn't make friends easily, so he's rather lonely. I think he likes the lack of formality here. It's one of the few places he can come and relax.'

'I've only met him a couple of times, but he seems very nice,' Tessa remarked.

Nell nodded. 'He is.' She smiled affectionately. 'Lamb by name and lamb by nature. I tease him with that, but I think secretly he rather likes having a reputation for being an old softie.'

'Something which obviously can't be said for Dr Nathan,' Tessa said ironically.

Nell looked up. 'Ah, do I detect a note of conflict? Have you two been getting off on the wrong foot?'

Tessa shook her head. 'He's against the family therapy group we're planning,' she confided. 'It seems that he and I may be crossing swords during the coming months.'

'That may not be such a bad thing. I always think a little friction makes life interesting,' Nell said with a smile. 'Dr Nathan is a very good doctor, by the way. Last summer Ben fell at school and gashed his arm rather badly. Dr Nathan was on emergency duty at the Health Centre and he stitched it for him. By all accounts he was marvellous.'

Tessa glanced up, eyebrows slightly raised. 'Really? He doesn't strike me as the cosy, avuncular type!'

Nell smiled. 'By the time I got there it was all over, but apparently Ben was brave and didn't cry. I think that went a long way,' she said. 'He obviously respected the boy. But that doesn't mean he's unfeeling.'

Tessa was silent. Perhaps Paul Nathan *was* capable of being kind and compassionate; maybe for some unknown reason, she herself brought out the worst in him.

In those first days Tessa was to learn a lot about the busy life at Laughton Mere Health Centre and about her colleagues too—all except Paul Nathan. He remained very much in the background and as much of an enigma as ever. She saw little of him in those early days, and when she did they exchanged no more than an acknowledgement, per-

haps a brief greeting. As far as Tessa was concerned this
was fine. She had neither time nor inclination for what Nell
was pleased to call 'a little friction'.

Beverley started at the village school, which was only a
short walk from the Old Vicarage. Each day she was taken
and brought home by Ben and Zoe, who had become her
devoted slaves. She was happy to share a tea of bread and
jam with them and then join them to play in the garden,
joining Tessa upstairs for a meal later, after evening
surgery. And so life at Laughton Mere settled into a
pattern.

The meeting to launch the Family Support Group was
arranged for a Saturday afternoon about three weeks after
Tessa's arrival. She and Rosemary had spent several
evenings deciding on what the programme should be. They
had decided to keep the introductory session as informal as
possible. Tessa was to give a short talk, explaining just what
family therapy was, and tell them a little about her own
qualifications. This would be followed up by a panel of
experts to answer any questions. From the subjects raised
they hoped to get an idea of the kind of problems they could
expect to encounter. Rosemary agreed with Tessa that the
participants should feel they had the maximum say in the
way the Family Support Group was run.

As the day of the opening session approached Tessa grew
nervous. What if the whole thing should turn into a gigantic
flop? Suppose the residents of Laughton Mere shared Paul
Nathan's view? Suppose they—like him—were to think her
merely an interfering busybody?

She didn't mention any of her doubts and fears to
Rosemary, who seemed convinced of the group's success.
She did voice them to Nell, however, as they sat chatting
over coffee on the Friday evening.

'Suppose nobody asks any questions when the time

comes?' she asked anxiously, voicing one of her many fears. 'Suppose there's a deathly hush and we're left just sitting there?'

Nell grinned. 'No need to worry about that if I know anything about the residents of Laughton Mere!' she said. 'But don't worry. I'll be there in the front row to ask that first ice-breaker for you!'

'Will you really?' Tessa asked in surprise. 'Are you really coming?'

Nell looked surprised. 'You bet! I'd like to see you stop me! I think what you and Dr Denning are doing will be invaluable, and I'm all for it. It's just what's needed.'

Tessa felt the familiar little spiral of nervous anticipation in the pit of her stomach. 'Well, I agree, naturally,' she said, her enthusiasm rising again. 'I only hope they do too. I hope I'm the one to do the job, that's all.'

'Of course you are,' Nell assured her. 'Not only do you have the training, you have the experience too. You've been through the mill.'

Tessa glanced up at her. 'Is it really that obvious?'

'Only to a fellow sufferer.' Nell smiled. 'And by the way, any time you feel like talking about it I can promise you a firmly buttoned lip.'

Tessa shrugged. 'It's hardly a new story and it certainly isn't a secret,' she said. 'I was too young—too starry-eyed. I didn't have the sense to see that Simon was too ambitious to accept the responsibility of a wife and family. He was appalled when he knew that Beverley was on the way. I was naïve enough to believe he'd get used to the idea, that once she was born he'd relent, but I was wrong.' She lifted her shoulders. 'I suppose he just didn't love me enough.'

Nell nodded wisely. 'As you say, it's an all too familiar story.'

Tessa sighed. 'I stopped blaming him or feeling bitter a

long ago. The truth is, we were both too young and naïve to have foreseen the pitfalls.'

'So what happened?' Nell asked gently.

'He left,' Tessa told her briefly. 'He said that family life wasn't for him.' She shrugged. 'That's all there was to it. I've never set eyes on him from that day to this. He didn't contest the divorce—didn't even come to the hearing.'

Nell nodded, making no comment—no judgement. Obviously it hadn't been as simple as Tessa made out, but she was far too wise to probe further. 'He helps with Beverley's upkeep, I hope,' was all she said.

'Oh yes. He's living in Yorkshire now—a highly successful insurance broker.

Nell nodded. 'And you? Have you ever thought of remarrying?'

Tessa pulled a face. 'You must be joking! Anyway, I have Beverley to think of. She's already missed out on so much. My life belongs to her now.'

Nell shook her head. 'That could be a mistake,' she said. 'Investing too much of oneself in a child can lead to heartache. You're young—and very attractive.'

'I have my job too,' Tessa said abruptly. 'That will consume all my surplus energy. I made up my mind long ago that I wouldn't allow another man to hurt me as Simon did. I shan't change it. That's one thing I'm *very* sure of.'

Nell got up from her chair. 'Well, it's an ill wind, as they say. You've certainly experienced first-hand some of the problems you'll encounter in the coming months.' Privately Nell wondered what advice Tessa would give to a young woman facing the same situation as herself. Standing outside herself, so to speak, could be something of a revelation.

As the hall of the Community Centre filled up the following afternoon Tessa looked anxiously at Rosemary.

'I never thought there'd be this many,' she said, her voice trembling. In her handbag were the carefully prepared notes for her introductory talk, but already her mouth was beginning to dry at the thought of delivering it.

Rosemary turned to her with a reassuring smile. 'I think we should make a start,' she said, looking at her watch. 'Shall we go up on to the platform?'

Tessa took a deep breath and nodded. 'All right.'

Rosemary appeared so calm and confident as she welcomed the gathered audience and introduced their new practise nurse and family therapist. She gave them a little of Tessa's background and training, then suddenly she was turning to her with an encouraging smile. The time had come!

To Tessa's surprise her voice sounded quite clear and calm as she began to speak. 'There are very few of us who do not belong to a family, or share our lives with others,' she said. 'And very few of us who are unaware that with the best of wills this in itself brings its share of problems.'

She had begun; her opening statement brought murmurs of agreement. She was encouraged, and as she went on it was soon clear that she held her audience in the palm of her hand. She was saying things they could identify with, voicing some of the doubts which many of them thought they alone held.

'Most of us grow up under the impression that being parents is natural and that we should instinctively know all the right things to do. And so we feel we have somehow failed when we come up against difficulties we find ourselves unable to cope with . . . Family life does not always consist only of parents and children. Many families have to include older members—sometimes those in failing health, who have somehow to be integrated into the family scene . . . In middle age there are the triple problems of dealing with adolescents and ageing parents as well as personal mid-life traumas . . .'

All of the things she mentioned struck a chord somewhere in the room, and she felt the warmth and assent coming across to her in waves as she spoke, her confidence growing. Finally she told them: 'We want you to feel that the Family Support Group, as we shall call it, belongs to you—all of you. We want to hear your suggestions on how it should be run. So if you have any suggestions—or want to ask any questions of either me or our guests, please feel free to do so now.'

Tessa sat down to a round of appreciative applause and there was no need for Nell, smiling up from the front row with Beverley beside her, to ask that 'ice-breaker' she had prepared. The questions and suggestions came in thick and fast from all parts of the hall, keeping Tessa and Rosemary busy for the next half-hour, when they broke for tea.

Nell and Beverley were waiting for Tessa at one of the small tables set out at the side of the room.

'We've got you some tea, Mummy,' Beverley announced exitedly. 'And a cake!'

'Congratulations,' Nell smiled. 'You were first class.'

'Could you see my hands shaking?' Tessa whispered. 'My knees felt like jelly!'

'Not a nerve-end in sight anywhere,' Nell assured her. 'You were terrific. By the way,' she leaned across the table confidentially, 'I'm not sure, but I think your opposition is here.' She glanced round. 'Over there, look. Isn't he the youngish one with the vaguely Gallic looks?'

Tessa hardly recognised the description but, glancing towards the other side of the hall, she caught sight of Dr Paul Nathan, chatting to Rosemary. Taking a fresh look at him, she supposed there was something vaguely French-looking about the wide mouth and jaw, the high cheekbones and slightly hooded eyes. The thought brought an amused lift to her lips. Paul's cold nature could hardly be said to match up!

Nell's perceptive eyes were on Tessa's face, noting the curve of her mouth as she looked across the room. She raised an enquiring eyebrow. 'So you're pleased he came to hear you, then?'

'What?' Tessa focused her attention on her friend again. 'Oh no, not particularly. I was just amused at your description, that's all. I daresay he came hoping for the pleasure of seeing me make a fool of myself!'

'In that case he must be very disappointed,' Nell remarked. She glanced towards him again, and then quickly averted her gaze. 'Oh-oh, don't look now, but he's heading this way.'

Paul had finished speaking to Rosemary and was threading his way between groups of people, coming in their direction. Tessa lowered her head over her teacup, hoping fervently that he would walk straight past. When his voice addressed her from behind she felt the colour rise in her cheeks.

'I think congratulations are in order,' he said.

She looked up. 'Oh! Thank you.'

'It all sounds very admirable—in theory,' he said drily. 'Let's hope it isn't a Pandora's box you're opening.'

'I think we shall be ready to cope with whatever comes,' Tessa told him, wishing she didn't sound so smug.

He smiled. 'Mmm. The impossible we do at once—miracles take longer, eh?' he quoted cynically. 'I only wish I had your confidence.'

'I think a family support group is badly needed here in Laughton Mere,' Nell put in quickly. 'And from the enthusiastic response this afternoon, I'd say that's a view shared by many.'

Paul turned his attention on Nell for the first time.

'Oh, yes, I'm sure you're right,' he said coolly. 'Any form of spoon-feeding is well received—until things go wrong and people start looking round for someone to blame. We already have Marriage Guidance and the Samaritans. Personally I can't see the need for any more do-gooders.'

Out of the corner of her eye Nell registered Tessa's exasperated look and wasn't surprised to find she was no longer able to keep her irritation under control.

'I might as well say why do you need preventive medicine when there are plenty of tranquillisers and antibiotics available,' she told him, her dark eyes flashing. 'Family therapy is also a form of preventive medicine, you know.'

Nell chuckled inwardly to herself, noting Paul's stunned expression. The barb had obviously found its mark. She decided the time had come to change the subject and, smiling brightly at Paul, she asked: 'Aren't you staying for tea, Dr Nathan? If so, why don't you join us?'

To Tessa's surprise he hesitated, glancing in her direction as though about to accept Nell's invitation, then he shook his head. 'It's very kind of you, but I really must be going.' He glanced again at Tessa. 'No doubt you'll want to mingle a little before the meeting finally breaks up,' he said. 'I'm sure there are hordes of people just dying to meet their new miracle-worker! I'll leave you to it.' He nodded to Nell. 'Goodbye, Mrs Orton.'

They watched in silence as he made his way towards the door, then Nell grinned at Tessa. 'Well, round one to you, I'd say. I see what you mean about him, though I must say that in your shoes I'd see him as something of a challenge. Wouldn't it give you enormous pleasure to wipe that aloof expression off his handsome face once and for all?'

Tessa looked deflated. 'Not really. I'd much rather he were for us than against us. As for his aloof expression,

I couldn't care less about it.'

All this time Beverley had been watching solemn-eyed from her chair on the other side of the table. Suddenly she spoke. 'Well I *like* Dr Nathan's face,' she announced. 'But why didn't he say hello to me?'

CHAPTER FOUR

THE FIRST of the Family Support Group sessions went well. Tessa presided, gently steering the conversation away from the ice-breaking trivial everyday gossip into the vital areas she knew these people needed to discuss. Gradually she managed to encourage the shyer members to relax and talk, and after the first awkwardness had worn off she found them meeting eagerly each week, talking fluently and frankly. As Rosemary had suggested, often just talking and sharing their worries was enough to reduce their anxiety.

The private surgery was another matter. This was held on Wednesday evenings. After the general surgery was over Tessa would change out of her uniform into something more informal. She always bought fresh flowers on that day too and arranged them on her desk in an effort to create an atmosphere that was as un-clinical as possible.

In the first weeks she found herself sitting alone and watching the clock as the hour ticked past, hoping for a casual last-minute patient as her brand-new appointment book lay empty on the desk before her. Each week she went home feeling disappointed and depressed. Perhaps the patients felt she was too young, too inexperienced to understand their deeper and more intimate difficulties.

It was on the fourth Wednesday, just as she was preparing to write off yet another wasted evening, that a knock came on the door of her room.

Looking up, she called: 'Come in.'

Thelma, the elder of the Centre's two receptionists, put her head round the door. 'I'm afraid there's a patient for you, Mrs Trentham,' she said apologetically. 'It's Mrs

Parsons. I told her it might be too late. Are you still consulting?'

Tessa's heart quickened. 'Yes, of course, send her in.'

The woman who diffidently presented herself a few moments later was perhaps in her late fifties and looked pale and anxious. Tessa stood up and went to meet her, pulling out a chair and drawing another up to sit opposite, so that her desk would not create a barrier between them. As the woman had not made an appointment she had had no time to consult her notes, but the name Parsons struck a chord somewhere inside Tessa, though for the moment she could not recall why.

She smiled. 'What can I do for you, Mrs Parsons?'

'Well, I don't know that there's anything you can do, really.' The woman looked unhappy as she twisted the strap of her handbag. 'I'm sorry to be so late—and you're going to think I'm silly, coming to you at all,' she said nervously. 'In fact if it wasn't for David you couldn't even call my problem a family one at all.'

'Suppose you just tell me what it is?' Tessa invited.

Mrs Parsons nodded. 'Yes—of course.' She paused, then added: David's my son—at university.'

Tessa noted that in spite of Mrs Parsons' obvious anxiety she couldn't quite keep the note of pride out of her voice. 'I see. Is he your only son?' she asked gently.

The woman nodded. 'He's all I have now. My husband died a few weeks ago—a heart attack.'

The missing connection Tessa had been searching her memory for dropped into place. Of course. George Parsons was the patient Paul Nathan had lost on the night of her arrival at Laughton Mere. 'I'm so sorry, Mrs Parsons,' she said. 'It must have been a terrible shock for you.'

Mary Parsons sighed. 'I knew his heart was bad, of

course—George had had other attacks. But this time it was so quick—so unexpected.' She took a deep breath. 'I've been all right really—coped very well until—well, until a fortnight ago.' Her hands were worrying at the handbag strap again, twisting it this way and that as she bit her lip.

'Yes, what happened?' Tessa prompted.

'Well, as I say, it was silly really. I was in the supermarket doing the weekly shopping. Everything was perfectly normal, then suddenly, without any warning, I had this—this kind of *turn*.' She glanced up at Tessa almost apologetically. 'Oh dear, it sounds so silly. It's so hard to explain.'

'Try,' Tessa invited. 'Take your time. Tell me exactly what it was like. And don't worry that it might sound silly, because there's no one else to hear but ourselves.'

The woman moistened her lips. 'First, my heart started to thump,' she began slowly. 'Immediately I thought of George and wondered if I might be having a heart attack. I went all hot and sweaty—and I couldn't breathe properly. It was terrible! I felt as though I was suffocating. All I could think of was getting out of there. I left the shopping—my handbag with all my money in it—everything! I pushed people out of the way and just *ran*!' Her lower lip trembled. 'I remember seeing the shocked looks on people's faces as I pushed past them, but at the time I just didn't care! All I wanted was to get outside.'

She paused and Tessa asked: 'Did you feel better out in the fresh air?'

The older woman shook her head. 'No—worse if anything. I just kept on running, blindly, like a hunted animal or something. I'd no idea where I was going, and when I finally stopped I didn't even know where I was.'

By now she was trembling, and Tessa reached out to take

one of her hands. She found it cold and clammy. 'What did you do next?' she asked.

Mrs Parsons shook her head as the memory flooded back. 'I go all hot and cold when I think of it now,' she whispered. 'What must I have looked like—a woman of my age running through the streets as though the hounds of hell were after me? I feel so ashamed—so humiliated. I keep wondering if anyone I know saw me.'

'I shouldn't worry about that.' Tessa patted the trembling hand. 'When you stopped running did you feel normal again?' she asked.

Mrs Parsons looked doubtful. 'Well, physically I did, yes. My heart had stopped racing and my breathing returned to normal—after I got my breath back from all that running, of course. But mentally . . .' She drew a long breath and went on: 'The next thing was to make my way back to the store. I'd left my car there, you see. I found my way back and sat in the car for a long time, screwing up my courage to go back into the store.' She swallowed hard. 'I was lucky; someone had taken my bag to the manager's office, so at least I didn't lose that.' She stopped talking and looked at Tessa as though trying to assess her reaction.

'And then you drove home safely?' asked Tessa.

'Yes.'

'What you had was a panic attack, Mrs Parsons,' Tessa explained. 'It was probably caused through delayed shock over your husband's death. It's quite a common phenomenon and nothing to worry about. It hasn't happened again, has it?'

The woman looked doubtful. 'No, it hasn't happened again, because I haven't let it.'

'What do you mean, you haven't let it?' Tessa asked.

'Ever since it happened I can't bring myself to go out—not unless someone is with me. And now that I'm on my own that isn't easy.'

'I see,' Tessa nodded. What Mrs Parsons was developing was a classic case of agoraphobia. She could have told her that she wouldn't have another panic attack—assured her that her fears were unfounded. But she knew that wouldn't work.

'How did you manage to get here this evening?' she asked.

'My neighbour came with me. It was she who suggested coming to see you. She came to your meeting the other Saturday, you see.'

'So at least you have a good neighbour you can call on?' Tessa said.

'Yes, but I can't keep putting people out,' Mrs Parsons told her with a frown. 'Not for something that sounds so—so neurotic and silly.' She began to twist the handbag strap again.'

Tessa smiled. 'Try not to worry about it, Mrs Parsons,' she advised. 'Worrying will only make you even more anxious. Try to ride it out. It will pass in a little while.'

'There's this problem, though, you see,' the woman said, biting her lip. 'It's David.' She looked up at Tessa, a mute appeal in her eyes. 'Oh dear, I'd better explain. George and I were to have gone up to the university to a special do they're giving—a sort of garden party. David was terribly shaken by his father's death, and now that he's only got me it's specially important for him.' She stifled a sob. 'But I can't go, you see. I've tried everything I can think of to conquer this feeling, but—but it's no use. I just *can't*!' She opened the belaboured handbag and searched for a handkerchief.

Silently Tessa pulled a tissue from the box on her desk and pushed in into the woman's hand.

'I'm sure your son will understand if you can't be there,' she said quietly. 'I don't think you should worry so much about it.' She waited until the helpless sobs ceased, then asked, 'When is the garden party?'

'At the end of term—in six weeks' time.'

Tessa smiled. 'That's quite a long way off, isn't it? Suppose you stop worrying about it for the time being at least? The first thing is to get you feeling better.' She picked up a pad from her desk and scribbled a few brief notes. 'Now, first, I'd like you to see your doctor. I'll have a word with him for you first if you'd like me to.' She looked up. 'Who is your doctor, by the way, Mrs Parsons?'

The woman gave her eyes a final dab and pushed the soggy tissue into her pocket. 'Dr Nathan. He's very good—he was wonderful with George and so kind to me at the time. But I didn't feel I could go to him about this because it seemed so trivial, and he's sometimes rather—well . . .' She trailed off and Tessa guessed that the word she hadn't liked to use was *impatient*. She smiled.

'Well, I'd like you to see him as soon as possible. And don't worry, I'll explain your problem to him first. Do you think your neighbour will come to the surgery with you, or would you like Dr Nathan to call on you?'

Mrs Parsons looked up hopefully. 'Oh, do you think he would?'

'I'm sure he will, under the circumstances,' Tessa said, mentally crossing her fingers. She made a final note. 'I'll ask him to call and see you tomorrow. Obviously you'll feel much more relaxed in your own home.' She looked up at Mrs Parsons with a reassuring smile. 'We'll have you feeling better quite soon, I'm sure.'

It was late when Tessa arrived home that evening and she found that Nell had put Beverley to bed for her.

'I knew there must be a good reason for your being late,' she said, meeting Tessa in the hall. 'And to tell the truth I really enjoyed putting a little one to bed again—reading her a story and so on. Any time you want me to do it, just say.'

Tessa sighed. 'You really shouldn't spoil us so, Nell. I'm sure it isn't good for us.'

Nell smiled. 'As a matter of fact there's spaghetti Bolognese on the stove—plenty for two. If you don't feel like cooking why not pop in and eat with me?'

It was sheer bliss for Tessa to have supper cooked for her, and after she'd been up to look at a sleeping Beverley she prepared to join Nell downstairs. She felt tired but contented. Her first consultation was behind her—even though it hadn't been quite what she expected. Going downstairs with a smile on her face, she reflected that although she had been in Laughton Mere only a few weeks she already felt she belonged.

The following morning surgery was busy. Three doctors were on duty, Rosemary and John Denning and James Lamb. Tessa found her own appointment book full too, but mainly with routine things. Her last patient was an elderly lady who was recovering from a knee injury, and Tessa had just finished changing her dressing when the door opened and Paul Nathan walked in, his face as black as thunder.

'May I have a word, Nurse Trentham?'

She met his cold gaze with equal iciness. 'Certainly, Dr Nathan. When I've finished with my patient.'

She took her time adjusting the tubular bandage and seeing the patient out, aware all the time of Paul's ill-concealed impatience as he sat at her desk, drumming his fingers on her blotter. When the woman had gone she closed the door carefully and turned to him.

'Another time do you think you could wait till I'm free?' she said coolly.

He brushed aside her request. 'The patients know I'm a

doctor.'

'Not all of them do,' she returned. 'It's an infringement of their privacy.'

His mouth set in a thin line of fury as his blue eyes glared at her coldly. 'As it happens I came here to ask *you* to refrain from arranging house calls without consulting me first,' he said.

She bit her lip. 'Oh. If you mean Mrs Parsons, I was going to speak to you about her. I forgot you weren't in surgery this morning, but I did leave a message at reception that I wanted to speak to you . . .'

He cut her off short. 'Oh? And I was supposed to hang around and wait till you were ready, I suppose?' He raised an eyebrow at her. 'Well, I'm sorry, but I didn't have the time. I've just rung Mrs Parsons to find out what it's all about, and it seems she'd perfectly fit to come into the surgery.'

Tessa stared at him in dismay. 'I hope you're not telling me that you've cancelled?'

'No—merely convinced her that she's well enough to come to me.' He held out his list of calls. 'Do you have any idea how many patients I have to fit in before afternoon surgery?'

Tessa swallowed an intense desire to shout at him. All her careful groundwork of the night before would be ruined by a few terse words delivered over the telephone. Mrs Parsons would certainly never make an appointment to see her doctor now. Her voice carefully controlled, she said: 'If you'd only asked me first . . .'

'I think I can manage my patients without having to consult *you*,' he told her icily. 'I managed without actually killing anyone till you came. I think I can continue without undue trauma to anyone!'

Tessa took a step towards him. 'It might just be possible that you're wrong this time, Dr Nathan!' Her dark eyes

blazed defiantly up into his. 'For your information, Mrs
Parsons came to see me last night. She had all the classic
symptoms of incipient agoraphobia, no doubt a delayed
reaction to the death of her husband. She's taken the first
step in trying to help herself, but in my view she needs
medication before she can begin. She had no one to
accompany her to the surgery, which is why I said you'd
look in on her.' She rummaged among the papers on her
desk. Finding what she was looking for, she thrust it at him.
'Here's the report I wrote up on her last night. It's what I
wanted to discuss with you.'

Paul looked at her coolly, registering the glimmer of
subdued anger in the dark eyes and the heightened colour in
her cheeks. 'I was under the impression that you were a
family therapist, not a psychiatrist,' he said with enfuriating
calm as he took the report from her. Swiftly he glanced
down it, his eyes narrowed and his lips moving slightly as
he scanned the words she had written.

'All right,' he conceded at last, looking up. 'This time I'll
look in on her, but in future perhaps you'll discuss the
patient with me *before* you make a diagnosis—*or* rearrange
my schedule for me!' And before she could reply he turned
on his heel and left.

As the door closed behind him Tessa allowed her
composure to dissolve. With an explosive snort she
grimaced furiously at the closed door. 'Isn't that just what I
tried to do, Dr know-it-all Nathan?' she said aloud. 'What
you need are some lessons in *listening*!'

She was still glowering ferociously at the door when it
opened to reveal Rosemary Denning. She stopped short,
her eyebrows shooting upwards as she caught Tessa's
furious expression.

'Oh dear! Have I caught you at a bad moment? Has
someone been upsetting you?'

Tessa slumped at her desk, feeling suddenly more tearful

than angry. 'Oh, it's nothing really,' she muttered.

Rosemary glanced behind her, then closed the door. She has passed an equally furious-looking Paul in the corridor. 'What did he do?' she asked. 'Come on, it was Paul who upset you, wasn't it?'

Tessa looked at her helplessly. 'I've put my foot in it again. Paul has just accused me of diagnosing one of his patients without consulting him. That and arranging his calls for him. And the awful part is that he's right, in a way.'

Rosemary sat down on the other side of the desk, folding her arms and regarding her friend calmly. 'You mean you really did those things?'

'No!' Tessa's eyes opened wide as she looked up. 'At least—yes, but I *was* going to speak to him—explain. He just didn't give me a chance.'

Rosemary sighed. 'Oh dear. Shall I have a word with him?'

Tessa shook her head. 'That would only make matters worse. He'd think I'd been running to you with tales.' She brought a frustrated fist down on the desk. 'Oh, why does he bring out the worst in me? And why is he so unsympathetic about what I'm trying to do here?'

Rosemary looked thoughtful. 'You'd seen one of Paul's patients—was that it?' she asked.

Tessa nodded unhappily. 'Mrs Parsons. I think she's going through a bad time emotionally since her husband died. Because she's slightly agoraphobic I arranged for Dr Nathan to call on her at home. But he was furious—didn't give me time to explain properly.'

Rosemary sat down, looking concerned. 'It's my fault in a way. I should have foreseen this problem. I think we should arrange to hold case consultations. If decisions are taken by consensus it will take the pressure off you. What do you think?'

Tessa brightened. 'I think it's a great idea.'

Rosemary stood up. 'Right, I'll arrange for a practice meeting right away.' At the door she paused. 'Oh, I almost forgot what I came in here for. Can you come to lunch on Sunday?'

'Both of us?' Tessa asked.

Rosemary shook her head. 'Naturally! Come at twelve and we'll have a drink first.' As she closed the door of Tessa's room behind her she looked thoughtful. Like all new ventures the Family Support Group was obviously going to have its share of teething troubles.

The weekend that followed was the first really warm one of the summer. In gardens around Laughton Mere sunloungers appeared, barbecues were trundled out and dusted off and the female population emerged in their summer dresses.

Sunday dawned fine with a clear blue sky and Beverley was up early, tugging the covers off her mother and pulling the curtains back excitedly.

'Look, Mummy! It's a sunshine day. Can I wear my bikini? Can we go to the seaside?'

Tessa sat up sleepily, blinking at her alarm clock. 'No, darling. We're invited to Auntie Rose's for lunch today.'

Beverley's little face fell. 'Oh, but there won't be anyone to play with there. Can I stay here and play with Ben and Zoe?'

'No, you can't. It would look rude.' As she saw the child's disappointed face, Tessa bit her lip thoughtfully. Since they had moved to Laughton Mere she hadn't had much time to give to her small daughter; Beverley seemed to have spent most of her out-of-school time with Nell and her children. She felt a stab of guilt. It really was time she devoted a weekend to her. She had promised herself that whatever happened Beverley should not be the one to suffer for this move. She reached out for the little girl and pulled her close, giving her a quick hug.

'Tell you what, you hop back in and I'll go down and make us breakfast in bed for a treat. You love that, don't you?'

'Ooh!' Beverley jumped back into bed and wriggled down under the clothes, watching as her mother slipped into her dressing gown. 'Couldn't we go to the seaside after lunch?' she wheedled. 'You did say it wasn't very far.'

Tessa sighed. 'We haven't got Granny's car to go in now, love,' she said. 'And it would take a long time on the bus. We'll go another Sunday when we have all day to spend.'

On her way downstairs she reflected that if she was to take Beverley out at weekends she would eventually have to find them a second-hand car.

When they arrived at Birch House Beverley was delighted to find Uncle John busily preparing the barbecue. He looked very businesslike in a blue and white striped apron worn over jeans and T-shirt, and Beverley danced around him excitedly, begging to be allowed to help. John began explaining what he was doing while Tessa watched, but after a few minutes they seemed to be enjoying each other's company so much that Tessa left them to join Rosemary in the kitchen. She found her putting the finishing touches to an impressive array of salads.

'Heavens, there's enough here to feed an army!' she exclaimed. 'How many people are you expecting?'

'Oh, there'll just be the four of you,' Rosemary said lightly.

'The four of us?' Beverley and I, James and . . .'

'And Paul.' Rosemary rinsed her hands at the sink and turned to look at her friend. 'Tessa, John and I would really like to see you and Paul getting along better,' she said quietly. 'Frankly, we both feel it's essential to the smooth running of the practice.'

Tessa sighed. 'I have tried, Rose,' she said. 'But it seems we have no common ground. It looks as though Paul despises all that I stand for.'

'I'm sure that can't be true,' Rosemary dried her hands on a paper towel and regarded her friend thoughtfully. 'There's something that perhaps you should know,' she said. 'Alison Moss, the last practice nurse, had a hopeless crush on Paul.' She shook her head. 'Well, no, I might as well be honest. It was more than that. The poor girl was head over heels in love with him.'

Tessa looked at her. 'I don't see what that has to do with me.' She gave a dry little laugh. 'I can assure you there's no chance of history repeating itself.'

Rosemary shrugged. 'I mention it because it may help to explain his attitude. I believe Paul felt guilty about Alison's unhappiness. He's a very compassionate man at heart, you know. He would never knowingly hurt anyone.'

Tessa bit back the phrase that leapt to her mind: *You could have fooled me*! Instead she said patiently: 'What you're saying is that he's deliberately showing me his worst side in case *I* fall for him too.' She laughed. 'Really! How conceited can he get? I'm sorry, Rose, but I can't see Paul Nathan and me ever seeing eye to eye. It isn't my fault, you know. I really have tried.'

Rosemary's face was unaccustomedly serious as she said: 'Nevertheless, Tessa, I'd like you to make a special effort to overlook what you see as his shortcomings.' Her grave expression relaxed into a smile. 'You're two nice people and I'm fond of you both. I really want this venture of ours to take off and be a success. I think it's up to you.'

Tessa didn't agree. It took two to make a harmonious relationship. In spite of Rosemary's attempt to put it tactfully the message was all too loud and clear to Tessa. Paul Nathan was here first and he was a partner, therefore he deserved the first consideration. If Tessa couldn't tolerate his attitude—if she and Paul couldn't get along, it looked as though her exciting new job might be in serious jeopardy.

CHAPTER FIVE

IT WAS a rather subdued Tessa who helped Rosemary to carry the bowls of salad out into the garden and set them out on the patio table. Smoke was beginning to rise from behind the rose-covered pergola that hid the barbecue from sight, and a moment later Beverley came running towards them.

'Uncle John's got the fire lit,' she said excitedly, 'and he's going to let me help him cook the sausages!' She grabbed Tessa's hand and began to pull her towards the pergola. 'Come and see, Mummy.'

Tessa allowed herself to be pulled towards the smoking barbecue. Suddenly it struck her that the haze of blue smoke was symbolic; for her there was a cloud of another kind over the day. It was clear that Rose and John had been discussing her failure to get along with Paul and it seemed that as she was the newcomer, blame for the discord between them was being laid at her door. She couldn't help feeling hurt at the unfairness of it. She really had tried not to offend the wretched man, and Rose herself knew that he'd been prejudiced against what she was doing from the start.

She sighed as she looked down at her excited small daughter, making an effort to shut her mind off from the problem—at least for the moment. But try as she would she couldn't shake off her resentment. However friendly and tactful Rosemary's words, the veiled threat was undeniably there, casting a cloud over the day she had looked forward to. However, for now she must try her best to forget it and make a pretence of joining in for Beverley's sake.

54

But as they rounded the end of the pergola she stopped abruptly. John was not alone. Paul was with him, helping with the barbecue. He must have arrived while she was in the kitchen. So far she had only seen him in the formal clothes he wore every day, but now, in jeans and a casual white cotton shirt, open at the neck, he looked completely different. The sleeves were rolled above his elbows, baring lightly tanned arms, covered with the same strong dark hair revealed at the neck of his shirt. Tessa stopped short as she stared at him. Like this, he looked younger and more approachable somehow. Certainly less formidable.

He was bending over the barbecue, gently blowing the smoking charcoal to coax it into a glow, but catching sight of her he straightened up. For a split second his eyes warmed with appreciation as they took in her crisp blue cotton skirt and white suntop, the slim bare legs and the rich brown lights in her sun-warmed hair.

'Good morning.'

His smile almost startled her. That too was unfamiliar and strangely disarming. It chased the glint of steel from his eyes and replaced it with a reflection of the sky—a clear summer blue. After the briefest hesitation she made herself smile back.

'Hello.'

He looked at the sky, his eyes crinkling at the corners. 'A lovely day; looks as though it's settled too.'

'Wonderful!'

Beverley had been regarding him with some interest. She too obviously found him more approachable in casual clothes. With none of her mother's resentment or inhibition she sidled up to him and slipped her hand into his. 'I'm Beverley,' she told him with a winsome sidelong smile. 'And I know what your name is—it's Paul, isn't it?'

Tessa stared at her daughter in horror. 'Beverley!'

But her exclamation was ignored as Beverley pulled at

the hand she held. 'Uncle John has some little fishes in a pond.' She pointed down the garden. 'He showed them to me. They're down there. Would you like me to show you?' Apparently oblivious of the warning signals Tessa was flashing at her, she urged Paul towards the crazy-paved path. 'Come on!'

His face relaxed into surprised amusement as he allowed himself to be led away. Tessa watched them helplessly while behind her John chuckled.

'Well, there's one young lady who doesn't stand on ceremony! Perhaps she has a lesson for all of us, eh?' He raised an eyebrow at her. 'Well, aren't you going too?'

Tessa hesitated, then said, 'Perhaps it might be wise. Goodness knows what she might come out with in this mood!'

'Well, don't be too long,' John called after her. 'This fire is almost ready to start cooking and I promised Beverley she could help.'

The ornamental pond was at the bottom of the Dennings' long garden. It was surrounded by willow trees, and Tessa found her daughter sitting with Paul Nathan on the little stone bench beside it. She was still holding tightly to his hand, regaling her captive audience with stories about Ben and Zoe and her new school. Tessa called her:

'Beverley! Uncle John says the fire is almost ready.'

'Ooh! Is it?' Beverley let go of Paul's hand abruptly and jumped up. Then, remembering her manners, she clapped a hand over her mouth and turned to stand gravely in front of Paul. 'Will you 'scuse me, please?'

He responded with a straight face, his eyes equally grave. 'Certainly. Thank you for showing me the fishes, Beverley. I'll see you later.'

As Beverley ran past her, Tessa stood awkwardly among the trailing willow fronds, not knowing whether to go or stay. Paul turned to look at her.

'She's charming,' he said briefly.

'I'm afraid she can be rather precocious at times. It comes of spending a lot of time with grown-ups,' she explained. 'I hope she hasn't been irritating you with her chatter.'

He moved along the bench, indicating the space beside him. Tessa took an uncertain step towards him, then glanced over her shoulder.

'Er—perhaps we should go back. Lunch . . .'

He shook his head. 'They'll call us. It's peaceful here—and cool.'

She sat down on the bench and glanced at him unhappily. This seemed as good a time as any to try to make her peace with him. Better get it over with. 'Unlike the atmosphere at the Centre, you mean?'

He turned to look at her, one eyebrow slightly arched. 'I suppose you could say that. You were right about Mrs Parsons, by the way. She seems to be heading for agoraphobia all right. I had to prescribe a mild tranquilliser, and for me that's like admitting defeat. I'd have much preferred to have headed it off.'

Tessa was taken aback. She'd hardly expected him to make the first move—certainly not to have admitted that he had been wrong. 'It's impossible to foresee that kind of thing,' she said. 'Obviously she's the type of woman who wouldn't let herself grieve. Maybe those around her expected her to be "brave". She glanced at his profile and added: 'I know you're interested in preventive medicine, and this is one way that a family support group can be of help—in sussing out those problems before they reach crisis point. As you've already pointed out, the average GP is far too busy to keep that kind of watch over patients.'

To her surprise Paul nodded in agreement. 'True. Rosemary said something similar. I understand she's arranged a practice meeting for tomorrow evening.' He turned to look at her. 'Was that your idea?'

It was a direct question, but the eyes that met hers were
no longer cold and hostile. Tessa found herself completely
disarmed by his sudden amiability, so that she returned his
gaze with slightly startled eyes as she said confusedly:
'*Mine?* No! Rosemary's—I only said . . .'

He laid a cool hand on her arm. 'Please, don't look so
worried. I'm not *accusing* you of anything. I happen to
think it's a very good idea to thrash things out.' He smiled.
'Obviously the FSG is here to stay, and I have to face the
fact that I'm in a minority of one.' He gave her a wry smile.
'Oh, and by the way . . .' he gave her a crooked little smile,
'Mrs Parsons was very impressed by your sympathy and
reassurance.'

Tessa could hardly believe she was hearing correctly. A
compliment—from Paul Nathan! Was he actually climbing
down? Then suddenly she realised what must have
happened. He and John must have had a conversation
similar to the one Rosemary and she had had in the kitchen
earlier. She felt her cheeks flush with embarrassment.

'Really? Thank you,' she muttered, feeling she should at
least show some gratitude for the proffered olive branch.
There was a sudden awkward silence between them and she
searched her mind frantically for something to say that
wouldn't sound fatuous. But a sudden shrill call came to
her rescue. She looked at Paul. 'Ah, I think I can hear
Beverley calling us,' she said, getting quickly to her feet
with relief. 'Lunch must be ready.'

Lunch was pleasant and relaxed. James had arrived by the
time they rejoined the others, bringing with him two bottles
of red wine which went well with the barbecued steaks
and sausages. Rosemary produced fruit and ice-cream for
dessert, which made Beverley's eyes sparkle, and when they
had all eaten their fill they sat sleepily on the lawn,
enjoying the sunshine. Tessa was drowsing blissfully,

listening to the subdued buzz of insects and quiet conversation, when suddenly Beverley's clear voice brought her instantly awake.

'Is that your car on the drive, Paul—the lovely blue one with no top?'

Tessa opened her eyes in time to catch Paul's smile as he confirmed that it was.

Her heart jumped into her mouth as she guessed what was coming next. She sat up smartly, opening her mouth to say something—*anything*. But she was too late to field Beverley's next remark.

'Will you take Mummy and me to the seaside in it one day? She says it's too far to go on the bus.' The child stood in front of Paul, her head on one side and her eyes large and innocent as she gazed up at him.

Tessa squirmed with embarrassment. *'Beverley!'* she admonished. 'How many times have I told you—it's very rude to ask for things like that.' Scarlet-faced, she got to her feet, gathering up her handbag to hide her discomfort. 'I think it's time we went home,' she said apologetically to Rosemary. 'Thank you for a wonderful lunch. We've really enjoyed it.'

Rosemary was trying hard to keep the smile off her face. 'Oh, please don't go,' she said. 'I was just going to make a cup of tea to wake us all up.'

'Oh, Mummy, I don't want to go yet!' Beverley wailed. 'If Mummy won't let you take us to the seaside can I have a ride?' she asked, treating Paul to her most irresistible smile. 'Just a *little* one—please?'

Unwilling to make a scene, Tessa shot her daughter a warning look. Paul intercepted it and said quickly:

'I'll tell you what, when we've all had a cup of tea I'll take you and Mummy home. How's that?'

Beverley jumped up and down, clapping her hands gleefully. 'Ooh—*lovely!*'

Blackmailed into submission, Tessa escaped with Rosemary to the kitchen on the pretext of helping with the tea things.

'My daughter!' she exclaimed when they were alone. 'I've never known her so precocious. I really don't know what's got into her today. She's going to hear about it when we get home, I can promise you that!'

Rosemary smiled. 'Don't be too hard on her. It's good to see her enjoying herself,' she said indulgently. 'Personally, I can't get over the transformation. When you first came here she was so nervous and subdued—like a little mouse. Obviously Laughton Mere suits her, and that must be a great relief to you.'

Tessa relented a little. 'She loves the new school and living at the Old Vicarage. Nell and the children are wonderful with her. I'm very grateful to you all.' She sighed. 'And, Rose, I will try as far as Paul is concerned, I promise.'

Rosemary poured boiling water into the teapot. 'Of course you will.' She shot Tessa a swift look. 'How *is* Nell, by the way?'

Tessa was slightly taken aback at Rosemary's sudden change of subject. 'Fine. Why do you ask?'

'Oh, no reason. I haven't seen her for some weeks, that's all. She's—well, is she?'

'Perfectly—as far as I know.' Tessa was intrigued by her friend's concern and waited for her to say more, but Rosemary picked up the tray and smiled brightly.

'Oh, that's all right, then. Be a love and open the door for me, will you?'

Thoughtfully, Tessa followed her friend out into the garden again. She had the distinct impression that Rosemary thought she knew more than she did on the subject, and her curiosity was aroused.

*   *   *

The back seat of Paul's Triumph Stag was just big enough for a small girl, and Beverley bounced up and down excitedly on it, the wind ruffling her curly hair on the short drive home.

'I like your car,' Tessa said. 'This is the first time I've seen it with the top down.'

Paul smiled. 'She's getting rather elderly, I'm afraid. They don't make this model any more, but I wouldn't like to part with her.'

They drew up outside the Old Vicarage and Beverley jumped out with a brief 'thank you' to Paul, running off in the direction of the garden, no doubt to tell her friends all about her day.

Tessa shook her head apologetically as they watched her go. 'I don't know what you must think of her,' she said. 'She's been so excited all day.'

He laughed. 'I told you, I think she's delightful.'

Tessa sighed. 'I'm not so sure about that. She can be very embarrassing sometimes . . .' She broke off, unwilling to remind him of Beverley's audacious request to him. It was too late.

'No need to be embarrassed,' he told her. 'Would *you* like a trip to the coast, by the way—next weekend, perhaps?'

Tessa shook her head firmly. 'Thank you, but no. We really couldn't impose on you. Look, I'd like to get things straight with you.' She turned in her seat to look at him. 'Rosemary gave me a little pep-talk this morning. I daresay John mentioned it to you too. I rather gather we—*I've* been rocking the boat, disturbing the calm—and as everything was fine before I arrived it rather looks as though I must take the blame. I'm sure we've both made a great effort today, but there's no need to go over the—top . . .' She bit her lip. It hadn't come out quite as she'd intended. Now *she* sounded rude. Anxiety over Beverley's behaviour had prevented her from choosing her words carefully.

Paul's brows gathered into a frown and the blue eyes hardened as he looked at her. 'I'm sorry you see it like that,' he said. 'But I can assure you that I'm not given to magnanimous gestures—particularly out of working hours.' His mouth set firmly and the steely glint returned to his eyes. Suddenly Tessa was reminded of Beverley at her most stubborn. 'As I've already promised Beverley that I'll take her to the seaside I'm afraid it's two against one,' he announced. 'You should never break a promise to a child, you know. Of course if you don't want to come with us . . .' He regarded her, one eyebrow raised challengingly.

Tessa stared at him, completely taken aback. 'I——Oh!'

'Quite! So I'll be picking you up next Sunday morning at nine sharp,' he told her. 'Oh, and by the way, you can bring the picnic if it'll make you feel any happier.'

He turned the key in the ignition in an obvious gesture of dismissal. There was nothing left, it seemed, but to get out of the car. Tessa opened the door and swung her legs out.

'And don't forget the practice meeting tomorrow night after surgery,' Paul reminded her, revving the engine ferociously. 'It might be as well to make some notes about the 'fors and againsts' of the FSG, because I promise you *I* shall!' He lifted a hand to her. 'Goodbye, Tessa.'

She stood by the gate, watching as the blue car pulled sharply away, sending up a cloud of dust from the dry road. She was so taken aback by this new facet of his personality that she completely failed to register that it was the first time he had used her Christian name.

Later that evening, after an exhausted Beverley had been bathed and put to bed, Tessa joined Nell in the living room where they shared a glass of her home-made elderflower wine, chilled to icy deliciousness. Tessa poured out the day's tribulations to her landlady, but Nell only laughed.

'What did she say when you scolded her about it?' she asked.

'She said that she liked Paul and wanted him to notice her,' Tessa told her. 'To her it seemed perfectly logical.' She shook her head. 'I'm seriously concerned. If I'm not careful she'll grow up into one of those awful pushy young women.'

'I wouldn't worry,' Nell said, taking a relaxed sip of her wine. 'Kids change a dozen times before they reach their teens. Anyway, why shouldn't she be positive and challenging?' She looked at Tessa, her head on one side. 'Now if she were a boy, behaviour like that would be thought of as "confident". Just because she's female it's labelled "pushy". I'm surprised at you, Tessa.'

Tessa laughingly agreed that Nell was right. 'I suppose women have played the submissive role too long for it to change overnight,' she said. 'All the same, no one likes a child who appears spoilt and cheeky. It might seem feeble, but I want people to like her.' As Nell smiled and shook her head Tessa suddenly noticed that she looked tired. She remembered Rosemary's obvious concern about her well-being and asked: 'You are all right, aren't you, Nell?'

The other woman looked up in surprise. 'Of course. What makes you ask?'

'Rosemary was asking after you. She didn't actually say so, but I got the impression that she'd been expecting a visit from you.'

Nell put down her glass and regarded Tessa for a moment, then she said: 'You and Beverley are obviously happy with our arrangement here. I take it you're intending to stay on—at least for a while?'

Tessa nodded, puzzled. 'Yes—if that's all right.'

'It's fine by me,' Nell told her. 'So, as you look like sharing the house with me indefinitely, I suppose I'd better tell you. I'm pregnant.'

Tessa stared at her, trying to hide her shocked surprised and biting back the obvious question that rose to mind.

Nell laughed. 'Don't look so surprised. I'm not exactly over the hill, you know!'

Tessa shook her head. 'Of course not. It's just—just . . .'

'Just that you're wondering who the father is,' Nell supplied bluntly.

Tessa's mind whirled. Suddenly she remembered Nell's friendship with Dr James Lamb and her eyes widened. 'It's not—not *James?*' she whispered.

Nell threw back her head and laughed. 'Jim? Good heavens, no! Our relationship is purely platonic. The poor old love would be shaken to the core if he'd heard that!' She drained her glass, the lines of laughter smoothing into seriousness as she looked at Tessa. 'It's not what you think, Tessa.' she said quietly. 'I'm having this baby for my sister Janet. She and her husband Tom have been married for ten years. Jan's lost three babies in that time—a stillbirth and two ectopic miscarriages, the last of which almost killed her. Last year her gynaecologist told her there was no chance that she'd ever have a child of her own—not by any method.' Nell sighed. 'I couldn't sit back and watch it destroying her—this desperate longing. I thought about it very deeply for a long time, then I offered my services.' She shrugged. 'You see, I'm one of those freaks who actually enjoys being pregnant. When I was expecting my two I felt wonderful, more alive than I've ever felt, either before or since. And the births were completely trouble-free.' She spread her hands. 'It wouldn't disrupt my lifestyle or my work unduly, wouldn't affect Ben and Zoe, so why not?'

Tessa frowned. 'I don't know what to say, Nell. It's your business, of course, but there are so many pitfalls.' She hardly liked to point out that Nell was now considerably older than when Ben and Zoe were born.

'We didn't take the decision lightheartedly,' Nell told her. 'We talked it through very thoroughly, and I think we covered every possible eventuality.' She smiled wryly, patting her tummy. 'Anyway, as I'm already five months along it's a bit late to start having second thoughts.'

Long after she was in bed, Tessa lay awake, Nell's disclosure nagging at her mind. During her family therapy training they had covered surrogate motherhood extensively, studying the Warnock Report. To Tessa it had always seemed fraught with difficulties of every conceivable kind; legal, ethical, moral, not to mention emotional. The gesture was typical of warm-hearted, generous Nell, and it could be the answer to her sister's suffering, but Tessa couldn't help feeling concerned about it and fearful of what the future held in store for her new friend.

CHAPTER SIX

SURGERY on Monday evening seemed endless. The warm weather had held and the day had been sticky and humid. That evening there was a constant procession of patients suffering from hay fever symptoms, sunburn, insect stings and other minor summer ailments. It was just on six-thirty and Tessa was thinking of changing out of her uniform when Thelma tapped on her door and looked in.

'Dr Nathan would like your help if you're free,' she said. 'He's got a distraught mother with him. Her toddler fell down some steps in the garden and cut his head quite badly.'

'Of course. I'll come now.' Tessa wondered as she made her way down the corridor why Paul needed her assistance; normally the doctors would refer dressings to her once the patient had been checked. But when she walked into his room the reason became clear. Through the open door of the examination room the young mother, her cotton dress stained with blood, lay white-faced and trembling on the couch, obviously recovering from a faint, while Jean, the younger of the two receptionists, was comforting the injured child, a little boy of about two.

Paul, who was at his desk speaking on the telephone, looked up as she came in. 'Ah, Nurse Trentham. Will you take Mrs Henshaw to your room and give her a glass of water while I examine her son?' He spoke briefly into the telephone, advising the hospital that he was sending a child in for X-ray. Replacing the receiver, he stood up, coming round the desk towards Tessa.

'Do you want me to dress the child's cut first?' she

66

asked, puzzled.

'It's all right, I'll do it.' He pulled the door of the adjoining room to and crossed the room to her, lowering his voice. 'I want you to talk to the mother—try and find out what happened,' he said quietly. 'She says he fell, but I'm not too happy about it.'

Tessa frowned. It was an all too frequent trend nowadays to suspect the parent when a child hurt itself. As a mother herself she could sympathise with the shocked young woman in the next room. 'Should you be jumping to conclusions?' she asked sharply.

'No!' he snapped. 'That's why I'm asking you to talk to her. That *is* supposed to be your speciality, isn't it?'

She allowed herself a wry smile. He did have a point. 'I'll do my best,' she told him.

She went into the examination room and smiled reassuringly at the girl now sitting up on the couch. 'Would you like to come along to my room?' she invited. 'Doctor is going to examine your little boy. He won't hurt him, but sometimes it's less upsetting for both of you this way.'

Mrs Henshaw managed a weak smile. 'I'm pretty useless, fainting all over the place, aren't I?'

'It's a very natural reaction. You'll feel better when you've had a drink of water.' Tessa took the girl's wrist and felt for the pulse. It was only slightly faster than normal. Obviously the worst of the shock was past.

Mrs Henshaw stepped down from the couch and allowed Tessa to take her arm and help her along the corridor to her room. Once inside Tessa offered her a comfortable chair.

'I'll open another window,' she said. 'It's so hot, isn't it? Would you like some water? Or I could run to a cup of tea if you'd like one.'

The girl nodded gratefully. 'You're very kind. Thank you.'

Tessa ran a cupful of water into her electric jug kettle, watching the girl carefully as she plugged it in. Her colour was beginning to come back, but the hands that lay in her lap still trembled as she twisted her fingers together anxiously.

'Children get very irritable in hot weather like this, don't they?' Tessa remarked conversationally as she got out a cup and saucer. 'I have a little girl of six myself, and I know she used to get quite impossible during heatwaves as a toddler.'

The water boiled quickly and it was a matter of seconds to pour it on to the teabag in the cup and add milk and sugar. She passed it across to the girl, then drew up a chair to face her.

'Want to tell me what happened?' she invited. 'Sometimes it helps to talk about it. It must have been a shock to see all that blood. Children's head wounds always bleed heavily. It always looks much worse than it is.'

The girl took a sip of her tea, then put the cup down carefully on the desk and buried her face in her hands, bursting into tears. Silently, Tessa passed her the box of tissues from the desk, knowing that tears were the best way for the pent-up tensions to release themselves. After a moment she leaned forward and touched the girl's hand. 'Mrs Henshaw, may I call you by your Christian name?'

The girl swallowed the last of the tears and raised tear-washed eyes to Tessa. 'Yes. It's Pam.' She swallowed hard. 'I didn't do it, you know,' she said, her voice trembling. 'I *really* didn't. At least—I did smack him. He'd been so naughty, you see. He'd been trying to get out of the gate all afternoon and I was scared he might get on to the road.' She bit her trembling lower lip. 'It's so busy where we live, you see.'

Tessa nodded understandingly. 'You couldn't have

known he'd fall,' she said gently. 'It was an accident.'

A fresh tear rolled down the girl's cheek. 'You don't understand—I've got to tell you. I didn't do it—but I *wanted* to; that's the awful part!' The words began to pour out in a torrent. 'I was at the end of my tether. I've got two more, you see. They're all under five and they'd been driving me mad all day. Just before it happened I got so furious with Darren that I wanted—actually *wanted* to hurt him! It's about all I remember clearly.' Her voice trembled as tears threatened again. Tessa picked up the discarded cup of tea and passed it to her.

'Drink that—and take your time, Pam,' she said gently.

The girl drank the tea and began to look better. Finally she put down the empty cup and pushed a strand of hair back from her forehead as she looked at Tessa again. 'It's such a relief to tell you. Just at first, when Darren fell, I wondered if I *had* done it—actually *pushed* him.'

'But you know you didn't?' Tessa waited, searching the girl's eyes.

'No. But don't you see—*I could have!*' The terrified eyes met hers. '*That's* what frightens me. 'Oh, Nurse, what can I do? Next time—next time I might . . .'

Tessa took both her hands. '*You won't!* Do you hear me? However stretched your nerves were you'd never do anything to harm your children, and deep down inside yourself you *know* that.' She grasped the trembling hands firmly and looked into the frightened eyes. 'Now listen—I'm going to suggest something to you. Can you get to the Family Support Group we run here at the Health Centre? We meet on Tuesday evenings at seven. If you could come along you'd soon find out that there are lots of mothers like you. You're not alone by any means. Could you manage to get a baby-sitter and come tomorrow?'

Pam nodded. 'I'll try.'

'Promise me?' Tessa looked into the other girl's eyes. 'Believe me, I do know how you feel, and I know we can help you.'

The cold fingers tightened round hers. 'Thank you, Nurse,' Pam whispered. 'I really will try, I promise.' She glanced anxiously towards the door. 'Do you think I could go and get Darren now?'

Paul had finished his examination of the baby when they returned to his room. Jean, who had been holding little Darren while the cut on his head was cleansed and dressed, put him down on the floor. He toddled grateful into his mother's arms, his tearstained, chubby little face now wreathed in smiles.

'I've dressed the wound with steri-strips under that plaster,' Paul explained. 'There'll be no need for sutures, but I'd like you to take him along to the hospital now for X-rays—just to be on the safe side. I've rung to say you're on your way.' He patted Pam's arm reassuringly. 'Don't worry. Babies are tough little devils. I expect he'll have forgotten all about it by tomorrow.'

Pam looked relieved. 'Thank you, Doctor. Shall I bring him back?'

He nodded. 'Make an appointment for a week today and I'll take the strips off. In the mean time just leave the plaster alone. It'll probably get a bit grubby, but I don't suppose his lordship here will object to that, will you?' He tickled Darren under his fat little chin and was rewarded with a wide smile.

When they were alone Paul looked at Tessa. 'Well?'

'Just the old story of a mother with an overwhelming workload,' she told him. 'Her nerves are in shreds, but that's par for the course with three children under five.'

He gave her a rueful smile. 'I bow to your superior knowledge, Mrs Trentham. What do you suggest?'

'I asked her to come along to the FSG,' she told him.

'Young mothers get bogged down with feelings of inadequacy and guilt, especially after an incident like this. They begin to think they're bad mothers, that they've failed—that everyone else is so much better at caring for their children than they are. It's only when they talk to others that they realise everyone makes the same mistakes.'

He perched on the corner of the desk, folding his arms and regarding her seriously. 'Just for the record—is the child at risk? To me, that's the real area of concern.'

'In a situation like that I suppose you could argue that all children are at risk,' she told him. 'But you can't start parting them all from their mothers and putting them into care, unless you want to light the fuse under a powder keg!' She shook her head. 'Things have changed so. Once most young mothers had their own mums close at hand—someone experienced to run to for comfort and advice. All too often nowadays they're isolated, far away from family and friends and afraid to admit their shortcomings. That's why I believe it's essential to form contacts—a lifeline.'

'Like the FSG?' He gave her a quirky smile.

She nodded gravely. 'Exactly like the FSG.'

He looked at her for a long moment, then stood up and walked across to where she stood. As he looked down at her she suddenly experienced an odd sinking sensation in the pit of her stomach. He was standing so close that she could smell the faint spiciness of his aftershave mingling with the more antiseptic aroma of the Savlon solution he had used on baby Darren's cut. The silence between them crackled with something she couldn't define and it unnerved her. She took a step backward, putting out her hand blindly for the door handle. Paul registered her uncertainty and felt a small stab of triumph. He might have capitulated professionally—at least for the time being—but he could still exert his masculinity.

'You know,' he said softly, 'it seemes to me that we're having the practice meeting Rosemary wanted right here and now. The others might as well have gone home!' He glanced at his watch. 'As it is they'll be drumming their fingers impatiently not a million miles away from here, wondering where the hell we've got to!'

'Oh, good heavens, I'd completely forgotten! And I haven't even changed yet.' Tessa's hand flew to her mouth as she turned away.

'You've no time for that now.' He took her arm firmly, steering her out through the door. 'We'd better go in and get it over with or it'll be midnight before we get home tonight!' When they arrived in the common room they found Rosemary, John and James drinking coffee as they waited. Paul made apologies for both of them and they took their seats at the table, where Rosemary poured them both a cup.

'I daresay you can both do with this,' she added. 'What was it—an emergency?'

Tessa began to explain, but Paul cut her short.

'No sense in beating about the bush. The meeting is clearly designed to talk me into a less obstructive frame of mind regarding the FSG,' he said bluntly. 'That being the case, you can relax. I admit that I was wrong about some aspects of it. Though I do still have certain reservations, I can see that it could take much of the workload off us, handled in the right way. And I'd like to go on record as saying that I'll give it my support as from now—on one condition.'

Rosemary managed with an effort to keep her eyebrows under control as she asked: 'And that is . . . ?'

'That for the time being we treat it as an experiment.'

All four doctors looked expectantly at Tessa, who nodded. 'I suppose that's fair enough, though it was Rosemary's idea in the first place, so it's her decision.'

Rosemary nodded. 'I agree that it's a fair compromise, and of course Tessa's job as practice nurse would still be safe even if the FSG folded. But I have to say here and now that I think the final decision should rest with the patients. If they think the Family Support Group is working and they want to keep it, surely you must agree, Paul, that we can't let them down.'

Paul nodded agreement.

'I have a suggestion to make.' This time it was James speaking. 'I've felt for some time now that this practice really should have a resident social worker,' he said. 'Now that we have the Family Support Group it seems even more necessary.' He glanced at Tessa. 'And if the experiment were to fail we would at least have some help available for those who needed it.' He looked around at the others. 'What do you think?'

John nodded. 'I think it's a very sound idea,' he said. 'In fact Rose and I have been thinking along those lines too. I'm sure Tessa would find the support that a qualified social worker could give her invaluable.'

They all looked at her, including Paul. Tessa nodded hesitantly. 'Well, of course, though at present there isn't really enough work to justify a full-time person. Perhaps we might borrow one on a part-time basis?'

John, Rosemary and James agreed that this was a good compromise. Paul shrugged and went along with the decision without objection. After one or two other items had been discussed the meeting was brought to a close.

In the corridor Rosemary caught up with Tessa.

'Congratulations!' she said. 'I hardly expected results like that in so short a time. What did you say to him?'

'Nothing,' Tessa said truthfully. 'Mrs Parsons' problem and the emergency we had at the end of surgery gave me two very good opportunities to point out some of the many ways in which the FSG can help—including in one of

Paul's pet areas, preventive medicine. But I have to admit that most of the compromise has been on his part. I can't take much of the credit.'

Rosemary looked impressed. 'Well, whatever it is I'm certainly not arguing with it,' she said. 'Keep up the good work!' She glanced at her watch. 'Can John and I drop you off on our way home?'

Tessa looked down at herself and shook her head. 'No. I still have to change out of my uniform. You two go on.'

Paul's Stag was parked in its allotted place in the car park close to the main entrance. He sat at the wheel, waiting. He had waved rather selfconsciously to John and Rosemary as they backed out of the space next to his in their BMW; also to James as he drove past in his sober grey Rover. Just in case they were speculating over his reason for sitting there he rummaged busily in the glove compartment as though searching for a favourite cassette.

He had to see Tessa alone again. Back there in his room before the meeting there had been an odd feeling of things unsaid—just what they were was a question he hadn't asked himself at the time, but now he knew he had to find out; for his own peace of mind, if nothing else.

As he waited he reasoned with himself. It was more than mere curiosity. It was important to know more about Tessa Trentham. He hadn't realised that the success of the FSG would depend quite so much on his co-operation. If they were to work together successfully they must at least make an effort to be amicable.

Satisfied with his own justification, he settled down to wait, and when at last he saw her emerge, dressed in the mint green linen dress and white sandals she had arrived in earlier, he wound down his window and put his head out.

'Tessa, can I give you a lift?'

She turned towards him, surprise in her brown eyes. 'Thanks, but it's quicker to walk, I think. You'd have to go round by the road; I only need walk across the bridge into the old village.'

'I thought you might fancy dropping in somewhere for a drink,' he said nonchalantly, 'to help unwind. It's been quite an evening. I'm going to have one, and I hate drinking alone.'

Tessa hesitated. To her surprise she found that his unexpected invitation flattered and pleased her. She had always hated being at odds with a colleague. She walked across to the car. 'Well, I mustn't be too long. I've left Beverley with Nell and I don't like to impose on her generosity too much.'

He leaned across and opened the door for her. 'Jump in. We'll make it a quick one at the Fox and Grapes in the village.'

The Fox and Grapes was Laughton Mere's oldest pub. It had been an inn since the sixteenth century. Tess took a seat by one of the deep-set mullioned windows, overlooking the village green, while Paul went to the bar. He returned with a pint of the local real ale for himself and a gin and tonic for her.

'It's quiet tonight,' he remarked as he settled himself opposite her. 'Monday evenings always are, I suppose.'

'Yes, I expect so.' She took a sip of her drink, glancing up at him over the rim of the glass. 'Oh that's good,' she sighed. 'It's deliciously cold. Thank you.'

He smiled and took a long pull of his own drink, wondering quite how one began the process of getting to know a person like Tessa. He didn't want her to jump to the wrong conclusions. Alison had done that without any encouragement at all! He already knew the basic facts about her. She was divorced—the mother of a small daughter. She must be about twenty-six; five years his junior. It had never occurred to him to wonder more about her, but now he found that he was curious. He watched her as she looked out of the window. With her delicately sculpted profile etched against the golden evening light she looked almost ethereal. It was impossible to tell whether she had suffered any trauma over her divorce. Life seemed to have left no tell-tale clues on the smooth oval face with its creamy complexion. Only the dark eyes were expressive —they gave all the clues to her feelings. He had learned that at least, having seen them flash with fire and dance with merriment—though he had to admit that so far he seemed to have caused more of the former than the latter. He guessed too from the set of her chin that she would be mulishly stubborn once she had made up her mind. Suddenly he surprised himself by asking:

'Does Beverley's father have access? Was that why you were reluctant about a trip to the seaside with me?'

He had caught her unawares and her head spun round, the brown eyes wide and stunned as they looked into his. After a moment's hesitation she said levelly: 'Simon hasn't seen Beverley since she was three days old. Neither has he expressed any wish to.'

Her voice was brittle and the clear brown eyes looked into his with a directness that he found disarming. He found himself looking away. 'I'm sorry, I shouldn't have mentioned it,' he said, reaching for his glass. 'It's none of my business.'

Tessa shook her head. 'No reason why you shouldn't mention it. We're perfectly happy with the situation,' she told him. 'Simon's having access would only have complicated matters.'

Paul glanced at her. Had he unintentionally touched on a painful subject? 'May I say that he doesn't know what he's missing?' he said impulsively, adding quickly as he caught her startled expression: 'I'm sure he'd have been proud of a daughter like Beverley.'

'You're wrong!' Tessa said bluntly. 'He wasn't interested then and he wouldn't be now. As far as he was concerned Beverley was merely a hindrance to his ambitions—and an unforgivable indulgence on my part. She was the perfect excuse for him to break free.'

He searched her face for a moment. 'You're bitter?' he asked.

She shook her head. 'No. I learned long ago that bitterness is a negative attitude. It gets you nowhere. Now I see it as an experience that helped put me on course rather earlier in life than most people.' She glanced at him and saw that he hadn't understood. 'Beverley is my life now,' she explained. 'At least for as long as she needs me. As for me, all *I* need is my daughter and my job.'

Paul was taken aback. She spoke with such determination, with the conviction of a woman who had set the pattern of her life long ago and intended to stick to it. Not for her the girlish dreams of romance that had driven Alison Moss to the other side of the world. He hadn't realised that he was staring at her until she spoke.

'You look stunned. Have I said something shocking?' Her brown eyes were clear and defensive.

Shaking himself out of his introspection, he shook his head. 'No, not at all. I admire your positive attitude.'

Tessa smiled wryly as she took another sip of her drink. 'Being left alone with a tiny baby dependent on one makes for positive thinking as little else does,' she told him.

Deeply curious, he found himself asking how she had managed to qualify, and learned about Tessa's mother and the major contribution she had made; also of the recent decision Tessa had had to make about her future and Beverley's.

'It was high time Mum had a life of her own again,'

she explained, 'so when this job came up . . .' She spread
her hands, and Paul nodded understandingly.

'It obviously means a great deal to you.' He looked at her.
'I'm afraid I must have seemed like a threat to your future,
with all my objections.'

Tessa's chin went up. 'Not at all. I hope to be able to
prove my worth professionally. I've no wish to be thought
of in charitable terms.' She gave him a wry sidelong smile.
'And anyway, I'm quite used to the male of the species
getting between me and my life. I think I'm equipped to
cope.'

Paul winced. 'Ah, I walked right into that one, didn't
I?' He smiled. 'I hope your unfortunate experience hasn't
destroyed your trust in men.' He raised an enquiring
eyebrow at her. 'Some of us are quite reasonable, handled
with care, you know.'

Tessa laughed, replying in the same light vein: 'My
grandmother had a saying: "Handsome is as handsome
does!" She finished her drink and looked up at him.
'Thank you, Paul. That was very welcome after a hard
day, but I'm afraid I'll have to go now.'

He tossed back the last of his beer and rose to his feet.
'Yes, of course.'

Sitting beside Tessa in the car on the short drive back to
the Old Vicarage, Paul felt a lightness of spirit he hadn't
felt since his student days. This evening he had learned
a lot about the young woman beside him. She was mature
beyond her years; she had courage too—the courage of her
own convictions. In other words she believed in herself
and what she was doing. Like him, she was steering her
own course through life. She was the first woman he
had met whom he could confidently consider a kindred
spirit and—he hoped—friend as well as colleague.

As they drew up outside the house he leaned across

to release the door catch for her. 'We *are* still going to the sea on Sunday, aren't we?' he asked with a smile.

She laughed. 'I'm afraid Beverley is looking forward to it so much that there'd be ructions if we didn't! Do you really think you can bear it?'

'Of course I can,' he told her. 'It might surprise you to know that I really do like kids, even though I don't have much first-hand non-medical experience of them.'

Tessa laughed. 'I think you might be wise to reserve your judgement until after Sunday!'

Paul's eyes were sincere as he laid a hand lightly on her wrist. 'Tessa, may I say that I admire what you're doing? I happen to feel very strongly that children should grow up with the security of a family behind them. You're making a big sacrifice in order to make sure Beverley has that security. I hope she'll appreciate it in later years.'

His eyes held hers and she was startled at what she saw in them—compassion, but something more besides —could it be admiration? Suddenly she became acutely aware of the warmth of his fingers on her arm. She admonished herself sternly. Just because he had extend-ed the hand of friendship—tossed a few kind words in her direction—there was no need for her to react like a star-struck teenager! She turned and opened the door.

'It's nice of you to say so, Paul, but I'm not really being as self-sacrificing as you think. Beverley really *is* the most important person in my life. She's all I'll ever need or want. When you love someone as much as that there's no such thing as sacrifice.' She got out of the car. 'Thanks again for the drink. Goodnight.'

Paul watched thoughtfully as she walked into the house. Somewhere deep inside he felt deflated and—to his surprise —envious. Beverley was lucky to have a parent to whom she meant so much. Tessa was lucky to be capable of such deep feelings—such firm convictions. He visualised the one-track, single course he had long since mapped out for himself. Till now he had always seen it as a gleaming golden road full of unhindered opportunity and promise. So why did it suddenly now appear as an empty, dusty track stretching endlessly towards a clouded horizon?

CHAPTER SEVEN

ON TUESDAY evening the group session of the FSG was crowded. Word had begun to get round, and more and more people were turning up at each session. Tessa suspected that for some the motive was curiosity, but she weeded those out by asking each new member to tell her in confidence what his or her particular problem was in private before she allowed them to join the group.

To her delight Pam Henshaw arrived as she had promised. She looked less distraught and seemed much happier this evening, and told Tessa that her husband was baby-sitting.

'We had a long talk last night and I told him about yesterday afternoon and the way I felt,' she confided. 'He's always thought staying at home with the kids a bit of a doddle, but I think I've managed to make him see differently now. After what happened yesterday he's promised to take more of a hand with the kids from now on.'

During the evening Tessa managed to isolate a small group of mothers with similar problems to Pam's. She put them into a corner on their own and introduced them to each other, suggesting that they each made a list of the others' telephone numbers, so that they would always know that help was at hand if they needed it.

The following evening at her private surgery Tessa found several patients waiting to see her. Things were beginning to look up in that area too, she reflected with satisfaction.

The first to be shown in was a teenage girl, accompanied

by her mother. Tessa invited them to sit down and established that they were Mrs Saunders and her daughter Sally. For a few moments they chatted—about the warm summer weather, about Sally being head girl at the school she would soon be leaving.

'I suppose you've taken your 'O' levels this year.' Tessa said.

'Eight,' Sally told her shyly. 'I haven't had the results yet, though, but I think I've done all right.'

There was a pause, then suddenly Mrs Saunders took a deep breath and said: 'Sally's adopted, Mrs Trentham. She's been with us since she was six days old.' She glanced at the pretty teenager sitting beside her. 'Now she wants to find her—natural mother. That's why we're here. We'd like your advice.'

Tessa noted that Mrs Saunders had shied away from the word 'real', using 'natural' intead. Her heart sank. This was a problem it was almost impossible to advise on. Hiding her dismay, she smiled at Sally. 'It's a very usual wish for adoptive children to find out more about themselves when they get to your age, Sally,' she said calmly. Looking at the mother, she asked: 'I take it you and your husband have no objection, Mrs Saunders?'

The woman shook her head, though she looked far from happy. 'We understand that Sally is curious,' she said, 'and we don't want to stand in her way. We've talked it over, the three of us, and we've decided to come and see you—be guided by what you advise.'

Tessa's heart sank even lower, though she did not allow her smile to slip. Somehow she must do what she could to help. 'I think I'd like to speak to you separately,' she said. 'Shall I start with Sally?' She looked at the mother. 'Will you wait in the other room, Mrs Saunders?'

The woman nodded and withdrew willingly, but Tessa sensed that the whole thing was worrying her deeply.

When the door had closed she looked at the girl.

'Why are you so anxious to find your mother, Sally?'

A dreamy expression came into the girl's eyes. 'If I don't I'll never know who I really am, will I?' she said. 'Mum and Dad are super, but they're so—well, *ordinary*.' She reddened and looked quickly at Tessa. 'Oh, I love them and I wouldn't ever want any other mum and dad, but . . .' she trailed off, unable to find the words to express the vague longings in her heart.

Tessa leaned towards her. 'You can't help wondering if you might have something special in your background somewhere—or something you should know about; is that it?'

The girl nodded. 'Sort of—but not *just* that. I want to know what she's like and why she . . .' she broke off, glancing at Tessa, 'what happened. I've got this photo of her, taken when she was just a bit older than I am now. She's so pretty and she looks so—so *nice* and sort of sad too.' She shrugged. 'I'd just like to meet her, that's all.'

Tessa sighed. 'Have you thought it through carefully, Sally?' she asked. 'It may seem simple to you now, but has it occurred to you that she might have other children by now; that she might not have told them about you? Perhaps she might want to forget about a time of her life that was painful for her. You see, you may be her natural daughter, but you'd still be a grown-up stranger to her now. How would you feel if you turned out to be an embarrassment to her?'

'Oh, it wouldn't be like that . . .' The words had rushed out, and the girl bit her lip to check them. 'I mean, I only want to meet her—just the once would do. And it wouldn't be hard to find her, 'cos I know her name.'

'How do you know her name?' Tessa asked gently.

'It was the photograph I told you about,' Sally explained. 'Mum gave it to me when I was sixteen—on my last birthday. It was in an old frame and I thought I'd buy a new one. When I took the photo out her name was written on the back.' The dreamy look came back into her blue eyes. 'It was like a sign,' she said dreamily. 'As though she did that because she hoped I'd find her again one day.' She looked wistfully at Tessa. 'I only want to see her—just the once. There's no need for Mum and Dad to keep making such a big thing out of it.'

'I think your mum was right to get someone else to talk to you, Sally,' Tessa said. 'It's a very emotional subject and only an outsider can see it calmly.' She smiled. 'Will you go and ask your mum to come and talk to me now, please?'

Reluctantly, the girl got to her feet, looking doubtfully at Tessa. 'All right—but you won't tell her not to let me, will you? Tell her I mean it when I say it'd only be once.'

If Sally had been dreamy and wistful about finding her mother, Mrs Saunders was just the opposite. Tessa could tell by her face as she took a seat opposite that the prospect of Sally's real mother coming into their lives had been causing her a lot of anxiety.

'Sally tells me she has a photograph of her natural mother. How did she come to have that?' Tessa asked. 'It seems to have been the trigger.'

Mrs Saunders sighed. 'Sally was abandoned. We took her first as foster-parents,' she explained. 'The photograph was with the other bits and pieces that were found with her. When she had her sixteenth birthday a few weeks ago we thought she should have it.' She shook her head. 'Now I wish we'd thrown it away when she became legally ours. Ever since she first saw it she's been obsessed. It's been nothing but Christine morning, noon and night,' she said wearily. 'Christine's her name, you see—Christine Markham.' She threw Tessa a despairing look. 'I don't see how we can stop Sally finding her mother, Mrs Trentham.

But are we doing the right thing? That's what we want to know.'

It was a tough one. Tessa put forward the same stumbling blocks she had pointed out to Sally. 'I think you have to be prepared for it to be a disturbing influence on all of you,' she said at last. 'Not knowing Sally's natural mother it's impossible to say what will happen. All I can do is to advise you about how to go about finding her. If you need help and counselling later, come and see me again.' She smiled apologetically. 'I'm sorry I can't offer anything more helpful. Have you made any plans for finding Christine?' she asked.

'Sally has,' Mrs Saunders admitted. 'She's written to a local radio station that gives out messages—you know, birthdays, anniversaries, that kind of thing—asking her to get in touch.'

Tessa shook her head. 'That's rather a shot in the dark. She may easily have left the district. Do you think Sally will let it rest if she gets no response?'

Mrs Saunders gave her a wry smile. 'Frankly, no,' she said with a sigh.

'Well, your best bet would be the Salvation Army,' Tessa suggested. 'They're marvellous at finding people anywhere in the world. Other than that I'm afraid I can't help until I know the outcome.'

Mrs Saunders got slowly to her feet. 'I'm just so afraid we'll lose her,' she said. 'Either that or she'll get hurt and blame us. Either way it looks as though we'll get the worst of it. I wish it was over and done with.'

Tessa stood up and held out her hand. The next few months obviously weren't going to be easy for the Saunders family. 'I'm always here if you need me, Mrs Saunders,' she said. 'Even if you just want someone to talk to confidentially. Come and see me again if Sally does find Christine, of course.'

When the woman had left she sat deep in thought for some minutes. Sometimes—as in this case—all one could do was watch people run headlong into trouble and wait around to pick up the pieces. She only hoped that in the Saunders' case there wouldn't be too many pieces.

On Friday afternoons Rosemary held her ante-natal clinic, with Tessa to help. Usually it was a happy two hours, with the waiting room full of expectant mothers in varying stages of pregnancy and the air buzzing with exchanged experiences, chatter about new prams, layettes, and knitting patterns. Rosemary loved her obstetric work best of all and she was usually in good spirits on Friday afternoons. But today she looked preoccupied as she flicked through the pile of patients' cards on her desk.

'Are you all right?' Tessa asked.

Rosemary sighed. '*I'm* all right,' she said. 'It's just that Nell hasn't shown up again. She hasn't been to the clinic since I confirmed her pregnancy. Last time I took her blood pressure it was higher than I'd have liked to see it. I told her that she should come regularly every month for her check-up, but does she listen . . . ?' She threw her arms up in exasperation. 'I might as well save my breath!'

'She seems quite fit,' Tessa said. 'And she assures me that for her, pregnancy and childbirth is easy. I've told her she should take proper care of herself. I'll talk to her again if you think she'll listen.'

Rosemary shook her head. 'It isn't just that. I don't like this surrogacy idea at all,' she confessed. 'Nell isn't as young as she was when she had Zoe and Ben. And she loves children so much. It worries me what will happen after the birth.'

'She has thought very carefully about it, Rose,' Tessa said. 'She'll have had nine months to have psyched herself up to the parting and the baby is going to her sister.

She won't be losing sight of the child completely.'

Rosemary sighed. 'Mmm—there are two schools of thought on *that* one too.' She smiled ruefully at Tessa. 'Well, nothing much I can do, I suppose. But I'd be glad if you'd do a little gentle bullying for me if you get the chance—get her to come for a check-up. The least she can do is to consider herself and the family she does have. I'd like her to go to hospital and have a scan—and amniocentesis. I don't have to tell you about the risks involved with a woman of Nell's age.' She sighed, flipping through the cards in front of her on the desk. 'Nell's isn't the only surrogacy case we have at the moment. Did you know that?' She looked up at Tessa, holding out one of the cards from the pile.

'No, I didn't.' Tessa looked at the card Rosemary held out to her.

'You might have wondered why this one is always accompanied by a friend. They both come in for the check-up,' Rosemary said by way of explanation. 'Mary Slade is married to a stockbroker. They have a beautiful home in the old village. There's no way Mary can have a child of her own—neglected fibroids necessitated an early hysterectomy five years ago. Jill Thomas, on the other hand, is young and healthy. She comes from the council estate. Her husband is serving a prison sentence for theft—he has quite a record. Jill has two young children and is desperately anxious about their future financial position.'

Tessa frowned. 'But surely surrogate motherhood for *gain* . . .'

Rosemary shrugged. 'There are ways round it. Peter Slade has invested money for Jill's children—unconditionally.' She sighed. 'The Slades have an awful lot staked on this child.' She shook her head. 'It's gambling with human lives and I *wish* I didn't have to be a party to it. There are so many pitfalls.' She sighed. 'If there were some foolproof

method of childless couples having a child that was closer
than adoption John and I would have done it years ago.'

Tessa thought about what Rosemary had said. Till now she
had always imagined that her childless state was intention-
al. She mulled over her views on surrogacy too, and her
concern over Nell's cavalier approach to her pregnancy.
Tessa knew that Nell was a great believer in natural and
alternative medicines. Everyone had a perfect right to their
own beliefs, and sometimes adhering to firmly held
convictions was more effective than conventional methods
simply because of the faith one had in them. She had seen
it happen often. However, Rose was right when she had
indicated that Nell was no longer in the first flush of youth
and she certainly should be taking more care of herself,
but Tessa wasn't happy about being the one to tell her
so. Nell had been wonderful to her and Beverley. The last
thing she wanted was to offend her by appearing to
interfere; after all, she was a relative newcomer.

It was as she was coming out of her room later that
evening on her way home that the solution presented itself
to her. Dr James Lamb came out of his room at the same
moment and the two of them almost collided in the
corridor. In his impeccably courteous way James stood back
to let her pass, apologising.

'I'm sorry, Tessa.'

She laughed. 'It was my fault. I was in a hurry as usual.'

'Can I offer you a lift home?' he asked. 'As a matter
of fact I'm going to the Old Vicarage myself. Nell has
invited me to supper.'

Tessa smiled. 'Oh, well, in that case, thank you very
much.'

As she got into James's Rover her mind was working fast.
He and Nell were close friends. If she would listen to
anyone she would listen to him. She glanced at his profile

as he went through the motions of starting the car. His greying hair and kindly face gave him the reassuring, fatherly appearance that made him so popular with the patients. He looked so solid and dependable. She decided to take the plunge.

'James, I wish you'd have a word with Nell,' she said.

He turned to look at her. 'Really—what about?'

'She isn't taking proper care of herself—coming into the clinic for her check-ups,' she told him. 'Rose says her blood pressure could be lower. She really ought to put herself first a bit more.'

He looked puzzled. 'I'm sorry, I wasn't aware that there was anything wrong with her.'

Too late Tessa realised her mistake. *James didn't know that Nell was pregnant!* But he was a doctor! How had he missed the tell-tale signs? Nell was quite noticeably pregnant now. Then she remembered Nell's penchant for loose kaftans, comfortable clothes that effectively hid her expanding waistline—also her boundless energy and healthiness, her lack of other pregnancy symptoms. Yes, she supposed it was just possible for James not to have noticed. She bit her lip and felt the hot flush of colour creep into her cheeks. She had committed the unforgiveable sin—betrayed a confidence.

To her horror James pulled over to the side of the road and switched off the engine, turning to look at her acutely troubled face.

'What's going on?' he asked, his voice uncharacteristically harsh. 'What's wrong with Nell? And why hasn't anyone told me?'

Tessa found her mouth suddenly dry. 'Oh dear,' she muttered unhappily. 'I—took it for granted that you knew. I daresay Rose did too. I'd give anything not to have spoken to you. Please, James . . .' she looked at him appealingly, 'can't we just forget it?'

'We most certainly can*not!*' James's normally placid face was as grim as his voice. 'You surely don't expect me to let it rest there. If Nell is ill, I want to know. What's wrong with her, Tessa? You'd better tell me, because Nell herself obviously has no intention of doing so.'

She winced. 'You're asking me to break a confidence,' she whispered.

'You can leave me to make that right. I won't give you away,' he assured her.

She didn't know how he would manage it, but she trusted him. 'Nell is having a baby for her sister,' she told him. 'She offered her services as a surrogate mother. She's getting on for six months pregnant. You being a doctor, I'd have thought . . .' She broke off, noticing the stunned look on his face.

'There's absolutely no reason why I should begin to think of such a possibility.' He ran a distracted hand through his hair as Tessa's startling revelation sank in. 'What in God's name made her embark on a thing like that?' he muttered, half to himself. 'And why didn't she tell me—ask my advice about it?'

'Perhaps because she anticipated your reaction,' Tessa offered. 'She'd have been sure to have told you soon. I mean, she could hardly not, could she?'

He sighed, still shaking his head disbelievingly. 'Thank you for telling me, Tessa,' he said. 'If it was a mistake it was a fortuitous one. And you can depend on it, she'll be taken good care of from now on. I'll see to that!' Tessa didn't doubt it for a minute. His face was set in firm, positive lines she had never seen before as he switched on the ignition and began to drive on. She gave a sigh of relief. It had been a bad moment, but she knew she could rely on James not to give her away—*and* to make sure that Nell followed the prescribed course from now on!

*   *   *

The fine warm weather held and Sunday promised to be even hotter. Beverley was awake at six. She woke Tessa by bouncing on her bed.

'Wake up, Mummy! We're going to the seaside today. Get up and make the picnic!'

Tessa groaned and looked at the bedside clock. 'It's much too early. Dr Nathan isn't coming for us for hours yet. Go back to sleep before you wake the whole house.'

Beverley crept reluctantly into bed beside her. 'I don't want to go back to sleep,' she said in a stage whisper. 'I'm not sleepy and it's too hot.'

'Well, try,' urged Tessa. 'Just for an hour, then we'll get up.'

Beverley wriggled, her small body charged with energy and excitement. 'Why did you call him Dr Nathan' she asked, 'when his name's Paul?'

'You know very well that it's rude for children to call grown-ups by their Christian names unless they're invited to,' Tessa told her. 'I hope you're not going to be as naughty as you were at Auntie Rose's last Sunday. If you are Dr Nathan certainly won't want to take you out again.'

'*Will* he take us out again, Mummy?' asked Beverley, her brown eyes gleaming with excitement. 'Do you think he likes us enough?'

The first vague stirrings of unease began to disturb Tessa's peace of mind. She loved her daughter dearly, but the child had such a lively, enquiring mind that it was impossible to guess what she might come out with next; especially when she took a shine to someone—and she certainly seemed to have taken one to Paul Nathan. All hope of further sleep quite gone, Tessa sat up in bed and grasped her daughter's shoulders, regarding her solemnly.

'Now listen to me . . .' Beverley's intelligent little face grew serious as she met her mother's eyes. 'It's very rude to keep asking people questions. It embarrasses them.'

'Why does it?'

'Because—because some questions aren't easy to answer —because the person might not want to.'

Beverley considered this carefully, then asked: 'Is it all right to tell people you like them?'

'Ye-es,' Tessa said slowly. 'But only once. Doing that too often is embarrassing too.'

The bright little face looked puzzled. 'I like it when people say they like me,' Beverley said. 'Even if they say it *lots* I still like it. Why don't grown-ups?'

'Because it's—' Tessa searched her mind for another word without success, *'embarrassing,'* she conceded weakly.

Beverley's eyes widened. 'Why are grown-ups always getting embarrssed all the time?'

Tessa gave up. Swinging her feet over the edge of the bed, she held out a hand to her daughter. 'Come on, we'll go down and have our breakfast. But don't make a noise. Nell, Ben and Zoe are probably still asleep.'

Downstairs in the kitchen as she cut bread and waited for the kettle to boil she viewed the day ahead of them with trepidation.

By the time Paul arrived in the Stag at nine o'clock, the Orton family were up and about. Tessa had seen little of Nell since her supper with James on Friday evening, so she hadn't heard the outcome of it. There was no reason why Nell should confide in her anyway. In fact Tessa rather hoped she wouldn't. It wouldn't be easy pretending to know nothing about it. She never had been any good at deceptions of any kind.

Beverley, who had been watching for the car from their sitting room window, ran out to meet Paul the moment he drew up, climbing into the back of the car and waiting eagerly for her day out to begin. With the picnic basket they had borrowed from Nell stowed in the boot, they set off, the sun shining down on them and the wind in their hair.

Beverley bounced excitedly up and down on the back seat. 'How long will it take to get there, Pau—Dr Nathan?' She glanced cautiously at her mother.

Paul laughed. 'Not long—an hour perhaps. And what's all this *Dr Nathan* bit? I thought you and I were pals.'

Beverley sat demurely on the edge of her seat. 'Mummy said it was rude and naughty, calling you Paul when you hadn't—hadn't *invited* me to.'

He glanced at Tessa out of the corner of his eye. 'I see—well, we can soon put that right,' he said. 'I hereby invite you to call me Paul. How's that?'

Beverley bounced back gleefully. 'Goody!' She leaned forward, her arms resting on the backs of the front seats. 'I've got my bikini on under my dress instead of my vest and knickers, Paul,' she confided. 'It's pink.'

'Have you? That will save time when you get on the beach, won't it?' Paul's eyes were concentrating on the road, but a sideways glance told Tessa that he was trying hard not to laugh.

The piping voice in the back chattered on: 'Have you got yours on under your jeans, Paul? Mummy has. We've put our knickers in that bag so that we can . . .'

'*Beverley!*' Tessa turned round sharply, eyeing her daughter warningly. 'It really isn't safe for you to lean forward like that. Sit back on the seat and fasten the seat-belt.'

Beverley's face fell. 'I only asked *one* question,' she pouted. 'I won't ask any more.'

At Wellesea they parked the car in a quiet lane and walked across the sand-dunes to the wide sandy beach. It was a perfect day, cloudless blue skies and a calm sea lapping lazily at the smooth yellow sand. Beverley gave a whoop of sheer joy and began to struggle out of her sandals and cotton dress. In minutes she was playing at the water's edge, happily digging in the sand with the wavelets splashing round her ankles.

Paul spread the beach rug he was carrying on the sand and threw himself on to it. Tessa followed, sitting beside him as he lay on his back, arms behind his head, gazing up at the sky.

'There's nothing to compare with a perfect English summer day, is there?' he asked, the corners of his eyes crinkled against the strong light. 'Trouble is we don't get nearly enough of them.'

Tessa shrugged. 'Perhaps if we did we wouldn't appreciate them quite so much,' she said. 'Believe it or not, I've already heard people complaining about the heat, and any minute now we're going to read about shortages of water, in spite of the torrents of rain we had in the spring.'

He raised his head to look at her, one eyebrow lifting. 'You're in a cynical mood today,' he observed.

She smiled. 'No, just a practical one. It's a way of life I can't seem to get out of.' Tension made her sound stuffy and smug and she knew it, but she could hardly tell him that Beverley's familiarity on the journey had stretched every nerve in her body. She put her hand on the lid of the basket and looked at him enquiringly. 'Would you like some coffee?'

He nodded. 'Great!' He sat up and began to pull his short-sleeved white T-shirt over his head. 'I don't know about you, but I intend to get some sun.'

To her horror Tessa felt herself blushing. Looking away, she rummaged in the basket for cups, muttering: 'Yes, of course—go ahead.'

Beverley appeared holding a long strand of seaweed, the bottom half of her minuscule bikini wet and coated with sand. 'Look what I've found, Paul!' She stopped short, gazing round-eyed at his naked chest. 'Ooh, why have you got hair all over your chest? *I* haven't got any—neither has Mummy!'

He burst out laughing. 'Young lady, your mother was right when she warned you not to ask questions!'

'Why—are you embarrassed?'

Out of the corner of his eye he saw Tessa's discomfort and said quickly: 'You know, if you were to look very carefully in that rock pool over there you might find some baby crabs—even a starfish or two.'

The brown eyes widened, lighting up with delight as Beverley abandoned the seaweed and ran eagerly off in the direction he was pointing. Paul turned to Tessa. 'How's the coffee coming?'

She poured the hot liquid from the vacuum flask into one of the mugs she had packed and handed it to him. 'You'll have to excuse her,' she said. 'She's been brought up in an all-female household. She isn't used to men.' She glanced up at him, relieved to see the smile quirking the corners of his mouth. 'I suppose you could say that you're a novelty to her, which is what makes her so curious about you.'

He laughed. 'Do relax, Tessa! And don't take what the child says so much to heart.' He grinned. 'Anyway, I think I rather like being a novelty.' He took a sip of his coffee.

Tessa smiled gratefully. 'That's a nice way of putting it. Most people would find Beverley's questions downright rude.'

'Kids *should* ask questions,' he told her. 'It's wrong to squash their natural curiosity.' He put down his mug. 'I'll go and help her look for starfish,' he announced.

Tessa laughed up at him, relaxing visibly. 'I warn you—you might find yourself regretting Beverley's *natural curiosity* before the day is out.'

But Paul seemed to find Beverley and her curiosity quite enchanting. It seemed to Tessa that he encouraged her quite outrageously as they played happily together on the sand. Before lunch the three of them bathed together in the shallows and to the casual observer on the beach they looked the perfect young family—the man in the brief navy shorts, tall, well built and lightly tanned, the girl in the red bikini, slender and shapely, laughing happily as they splashed in the warm sea with the happy little dark-haired girl.

It was a sleepy, sun-tanned Beverley who curled up on the back seat of the Stag early that evening as the three prepared for the drive home. Tessa watched as Paul folded the beach rug to make a pillow for her, tucking it tenderly under her head as he settled her for the drive home. Beverley looked drowsily up at him.

'Paul, why haven't I got a daddy?' she asked suddenly.

Paul shook his head. 'Not everyone has,' he told her. 'I haven't, for a start.'

'Children have, though,' she told him gravely. 'Everyone in my class at school has—all except me.' She looked up at him, the brown eyes appealing. 'It must be nice to have a daddy. I wish I had one.' She stifled a yawn. 'Will you be my daddy, please, Paul? I'd *really* like that.'

CHAPTER EIGHT

BLISSFULLY unaware of the havoc she had caused in the minds of the two people sitting in the front of the car, Beverley fell asleep almost at once.

Tessa was silent. What could she say? To apologise yet again would make her look ridiculous. It was no use trying to explain to a six-year-old, either, that one didn't ask comparative strangers to become one's father. Odd that Beverley should choose this particular moment to enquire for the first time about the absence of her father. Tessa had always know the question would arise one day, but she could hardly have visualised being faced with it today—and in this manner. She chewed the inside of her lip. Trust her daughter to employ such devastating timing! She asked herself what her mother's reaction would have been and guessed that she would probably have laughed. Perhaps that was the best attitude to take. She took a sideways look at Paul's profile. He looked thoughtful—almost grim as he concentrated on the road ahead. Clearly he did not see it as a laughing matter.

But Paul's preoccupation was with himself rather than with Tessa and her daughter. He was discovering some surprising things about himself. The little dark-eyed girl in the back of his car had stirred a new emotion in him—one he had never experienced before. He'd never had much to do with children, except as patients. Although he could usually establish a fairly good rapport with them he had never felt any great affinity with a child before. In fact, until he met Beverley he would quite probably have described them as noisy and undisciplined and demanding. He found Tessa's child's clear-eyed frankness oddly engaging. He felt a small ache of pity for her tender years and her lack of a settled family home. He knew all too well what *that* felt like. Although he was grateful to the spartan upbringing that had resulted in his strength and independence, he would not wish the privations of his own childhood on any other child. At least Beverley had a mother who cared for her. As for her innocent request, he felt strangely touched and flattered by it. The implication it carried—that was causing her mother such disquiet at that very moment—had quite escaped his notice.

He turned to look at Tessa, sitting at his side. The sun had touched her skin, warming it with a light golden glow, and he noticed a sprinkling of coppery freckles across her nose that hadn't been there before. Her normally smooth brown hair was ruffled by the breeze as the open-topped car sped along, giving her a care-free appearance. Her pensive expression belied this, however, and he found himself speculating over it.

Feeling his eyes on her, Tessa turned. 'Beverley is far too young to realise the implication of what she said, of course.' She had unwittingly answered the question in his mind. Meeting his surprised eyes, she immediately looked away again, her colour rising.

Paul frowned. 'The implication? I'm sorry, I don't . . .' Suddenly the reason for Tessa's discomfort dawned on him. '*Oh!* I see what you mean. Well, of course she's too young. I never for one moment thought . . .' He reached out to touch one of the brown hands lying in her lap. 'Look, Tessa, you might as well face the fact that Beverley is growing up fast. She's a bright, intelligent child who demands truthful answers to her questions. The only sensible thing to do is to give her those answers and try to laugh any implications off, otherwise you're going to find yourself unable to make new friends of the opposite sex without finding yourself in a permanent state of embarrassment.'

Tessa sighed uneasily. 'I know. And it's good of you to see it that way.'

'Nothing good about it.' His eyes were on the road ahead. 'It's just common sense, that's all.'

But in spite of Paul's reassurance Tessa remained quiet for the rest of the journey, preoccupied with her own thoughts. Beverley's behaviour had put her at a dis-advantage, and however detached Paul might be, pretending he hadn't taken in the full implication, she resented the feeling. She decided there and then not to accept another invitation from him. He would probably feel obliged to ask her out again just to prove his point. The thought was deeply humiliating and brought the colour flooding back to her cheeks.

When they drew up outside the Old Vicarage Paul switched off the engine and turned to look into the back of the car. Beverley was still fast asleep. He smiled at Tessa.

'She's well away. It's a shame to disturb her. Shall I carry her in for you?'

She shook her head. 'It's all right, I can manage, thank you.'

The stiffness of her tone made him look searchingly at her. 'Is something wrong? You're not still worrying about what she said, are you?'

Tessa shook her head, trying to smile. 'Of course not. I'm very grateful to you. Beverley's had a lovely day. It's some time since she had an outing. I really must try to find more time to be with her.' While she was speaking she was gathering up her bag and the holdall containing Beverley's things. Paul laid a hand on her arm.

'There *is* something wrong, isn't there? Do you want to talk about it?'

She sighed. 'No, I . . .' She tried to withdraw her arm from under his hand, but his grip on it tightened while his other hand reached out to turn her face towards him.

'Listen, Tessa. *I* had a good time today too. I really enjoyed myself, and I'd like to thank *you*.' He gestured with a look towards the back seat. '*And* that little lady too, of course. She's full of personality.'

Tessa looked at him warily. 'You don't have to pander to my feelings, Paul. I'm not a child and I . . .' Her words were lost as his mouth covered hers. His kiss was slow and deliberate—and just a little longer than a casual salute. When he raised his head to look at her, her eyes shone luminously in the fading light.

'Does that do anything to prove my sincerity?' he asked her quietly. 'I must say you're a very difficult lady to convince.'

Tessa swallowed hard. Inside her chest her heart was drumming and there was a sinking feeling in the pit of her stomach. Suddenly it occurred to her that Paul was the first man she had allowed to kiss her since Simon and she had parted. Something else occurred to her too—something infinitely disturbing. Paul was the first man she had *wanted* to kiss her since Simon and she had parted.

'Well?' The fingers that held her chin gently shook her head from side to side.

She smiled, avoiding his probing eyes. 'I must go now, Paul,' she said shakily, firmly extricating herself from his arms. 'I must get Beverley to bed. There's school in the morning.'

He let her go abruptly, sensing her withdrawal and

misinterpreting it. 'Yes—yes, of course.'

When Beverley was safely in bed Tessa found she could not settle. Her own thoughts were far too disturbing. Going downstairs, she knocked on Nell's door and was immediately invited in.

'Nice day at the beach?' The older woman asked as she poured two glasses of wine.

Tessa nodded. 'Beverley was in her element. She adores the seaside. It was good to see her enjoying herself.'

Nell shot her a speculative look. 'So Beverley enjoyed it. What about you?'

'Yes, I enjoyed it too.' Tess's hesitation lasted just a fraction too long and she completely failed to get any enthusiasm into her tone.

Nell shook her head. 'Oh dear, that sounds ominous. Want to talk about it?'

Tessa sighed. 'I'm afraid my daughter is rather too free with her admiration. She's taken a fancy to Dr Nathan. I seem to spend most of my time apologising for her.'

Nell grinned. 'I don't really see why you should apologise for the child's obvious hero-worship.' She chuckled. 'Though I can imagine what you mean. Children of Beverley's age have few inhibitions, and their honesty can be downright alarming at times. The best thing to do is to laugh it off.' She looked at Tessa's strained face as she sipped at her wine. 'What did she say that was so awful?'

'Only asked Paul if he would be her daddy,'

Nell roared with laughter. 'Oh, lord! How did you cope with that one?'

'Badly,' Tessa told her wryly. 'Paul was quick to reassure me. He even pretended he hadn't understood what she meant. But he has no experience of children apart from in the surgery. Heaven only knows what he was really thinking. Probably that I've trained her to find me a new husband!'

Nell's smile vanished. 'Oh, Tessa! You really let it get to you, didn't you? For heaven's sake, girl—he's an adult, intelligent man, not a moron! I daresay he saw the whole thing as a rather flattering joke.'

Tessa tossed down the last of her wine in an impatient gesture. 'At my expense! Maybe I'm over-sensitive, Nell, but I've always felt vulnerable as a single parent. A lot of men seem to think . . .'

'That you're a seething mass of frustrated womanhood, ready and eager to leap into bed with the first male who crosses your path?' Nell finished for her. She chuckled. 'I'm afraid that's one of the crosses we all have to bear. And like all the others, it's better laughed off, believe me. Otherwise you end up suspicious and wary—maybe even missing the chance of a really rewarding relationship.'

Tessa looked at her friend. 'Oh, I daresay you're right.'

'I *am* right!' Nell leaned forward. 'You don't have to live like a nun, Tessa, even if you don't want to marry again. You should get out and about more, you know. A child and a job aren't enough for a young woman of your age.' She got up and poured Tessa another glass of wine. 'By the way, I told James about the baby when he came to supper the other night.'

Tessa looked up, her own worries temporarily forgotten. 'You—*told* him?'

Nell nodded. 'Silly old duffer! You'd have thought he'd have guessed by now, wouldn't you? It seems to me that doctors are the least observant people when it comes to those closest to them.'

'What did he say?' Tessa asked.

Nell smiled wryly. 'Oh, he tried hard not to look shocked, bless him. Then he startled going on about all the risks—about ante-natal check-ups and boring things like that.'

'He did have a point, you know,' Tessa told her, seizing her opportunity. 'I haven't seen you once at Rose's clinic.'

'And you won't either,' Nell told her decisively. 'It's bad enough having that young midwife Jenny Cairns calling round every so often with her oh-so-tactful words of advice. I've told her that I shall go on drinking my raspberry leaf tea, meditating and doing my yoga exercises. They'll stand me in good stead, just as they did before.'

'I know Rosemary and Jenny would have been happier if you'd been for a scan,' Tessa told her. 'And maybe amniocentesis—just to be on the safe side. They're both of them only thinking of your health and the baby's.

But Nell only smiled serenely. 'Just you tell those two ladies that I'll see them when I get those first pains and not before. I'm having the baby right here at home too. They won't get me into the Oakmoor GP Unit for delivery. I don't believe in drugs and technology.'

'But surely surrogacy employs a certain amount of technology,' Tessa argued. 'If you were prepared to . . .' She broke off as Nell shook her head.

'There was no technology employed in this pregnancy,' she said frankly. 'The three of us discussed it at some length and we decided unanimously that the baby should be conceived naturally so that it should be as close to Janet's own as it possibly could. So I can see no reason to start throwing myself into the space age at this stage in the proceedings!' She patted the growing globe of her abdomen. 'I can feel my baby moving, Tessa. He's as strong and healthy as I am. I'd *know* if there were anything wrong with him, so don't waste any more of your precious time worrying about me.'

Her tone was totally positive and Tessa knew that

say what she might there would be no changing Nell's mind. However, she couldn't help noticing one tiny point: Nell had unconsciously used the word *my* when she referred to the baby. Could Rose have been right about a possible change of heart? She hoped not.

In the weeks that followed Tessa avoided being alone with Paul. He in his turn made no attempt to see her or ask her out again, and Tessa was relieved. She had refused to admit to herself that she was attracted to Paul. The reason was far too deep and complex to go into and she shied away from giving it too much thought, half afraid of what might emerge. Paul's coolness gave her the perfect excuse to shelve the whole issue.

The more she thought about it the more she realised that the situation on that Sunday evening had been bungled. Obviously Paul hadn't meant to kiss her. It had been an impulsive action which he'd quite clearly since regretted. Tessa remembered the unfortunate Alison whose place she had taken, and shuddered. Was Paul afraid of being lumbered with another clinging woman? She longed for an opportunity to reassure him on this point, but could see no way of engineering one. When they met during the course of their work Paul was pleasant but distinctly professional. This was obviously the way he intended things to stay, and Tessa told herself determinedly that she would see to it that they did.

She'd had a frank talk to Beverley, explaining as best she could that it simply wasn't done to invite comparatively strange men to become part of the family, however much one liked them, and although the child had seemed disappointed, Tessa felt fairly confident that she understood and would make no further embarrassing gaffes.

*   *   *

The part-time social worker, on loan to the practice by the local health authority, arrived one morning about three weeks later. He was an athletic-looking young man with a shock of curling brown hair and a Liverpool accent. Thelma showed him into Tessa's room just after morning surgery ended, and without ceremony he perched on the corner of her desk and introduced himself as Kevin Donaghue. Over coffee Tessa told him a little about the Family Support Group and of the kind of problems she had so far encountered. But almost immediately she began to wonder whether she had made the right decision in agreeing to the experiment. Immediately it was obvious to her that Kevin Donaghue's approach was very different from her own. Seeing her doubtful expression he said:

'I'm not here to interfere, you know. Please don't think that.' He smiled at her. 'I thought I'd just sit in on your group sessions and maybe look in a couple of times a week—just to give you any advice you might need. I'm sure you'll agree that it'd be good to have the support of someone qualified. You must have felt the need for a substantial back-up at times.'

Tessa flushed. 'Our Family Support Group is very informal—and anyway, I *do* happen to be qualified, Mr Donaghue,' she reminded him.

He treated her to his most beguiling smile. 'Ah, *sure* you are—in your own field. But you could get just the tiniest bit out of your depth, now couldn't you? And wouldn't that be where I'd come in? Oh, and by the way, please call me Kev, everyone does.'

Slightly disarmed by his blatant charm, Tessa nodded. 'Oh—yes.'

'Yes, *Kev*,' he prompted, his head on one side.

'Er—yes—*Kev*. It's just that a good many of these people come to me simply for informal advice—and in confidence. I'd hate them to think that I was passing on information to the DHSS about them. I wouldn't want any of these cases to be taken out of my hands.'

He shook his head at her. 'Ah, surely you don't think I'd do that? I'm here to advise and help,' he said soothingly. 'In case, as I said, you get bogged down, so to speak.' He looked at his watch. 'Look, it's after twelve. What are you planning to do for lunch?'

Tessa shrugged. 'Well, I was just going to grab a glass of milk and a sandwich here and work through.'

'Tut, tut, tut!' He shook his head reprovingly. 'Don't you know that's the quickest way to ruin your digestion?' Again he peered at the large digital watch he wore. 'I saw a nice little pub in the village—the Fox and Grapes, was it? Suppose we meet in there in half an hour?'

By this time he was standing at the door, the handle in his hand. Tessa tried hard to think of an excuse, but he seemed to take her hesitation for assent. 'That's settled, then. I'll look forward to it—see you later.' And with a wave of his hand he was gone.

Tessa, her mouth still half open, stared at the space he had vacated. Was Kevin Donaghue's 'help' going to turn out to be more like sabotage? Her relationship with most of the people who came for advice was tenuous and delicate at best. Kev Donaghue reminded her of a friendly Labrador puppy, all eager bounce and good intentions. Would he scare the more faint-hearted away? But perhaps she was judging him too quickly, she told herself as she began to tidy her desk. After all, as he had pointed out to her, he *was* a qualified social worker. And it was only an experiment, after all. If she had doubts about its success she could always mention them at the next practice meeting.

The bar at the Fox and Grapes was crowded, but Tessa

soon spotted Kevin Donaghue. He was sitting on a stool at the bar, chatting to the pretty blonde barmaid. When he saw her he waved, beckoning her over.

'Hi, Tessa! What are you drinking?'

'Just mineral water for me, please,' she told him. 'I don't drink in the middle of the day. Not working days, anyway.'

He pulled a face. 'I take it you do *eat?*'

The barmaid giggled and handed Tessa a handwritten menu. She glanced at it and ordered soup and a salad sandwich. Kevin ordered a pint of the local ale and a ploughman's lunch, instructing the girl to be 'heavy on the cheese'.

'I always try to stoke up well at midday,' he told her as they moved to one of the tables. 'Never know what you might have to face in this job.' He pulled out a chair for her. 'Violence to the person is not unknown,' he added, half jokingly.

'So I've heard.' Tessa looked at him. 'But I daresay there is a lighter side.'

He shrugged. 'Well, let's just say that there are a lot worse places than Oakmoor.' He leaned forward. 'Now, suppose you tell me something about yourself?'

Tessa coloured, slightly taken aback. She hadn't anticipated this as part of the arrangement. Sensing her reluctance, Kevin added quickly:

'Strictly off the record, of course. It's just that I like to be on good terms with the people I work with. I always think it makes for better co-operation. Oh, and while we're on the subject, can you let me have your home address and phone number?' He pulled out a notebook and looked up at her expectantly.

'Is that really necessary?' she asked.

'Well, just as you please,' he said. 'But in our kind of work the worst crises always seem to occur outside office hours, don't you find?'

'In that case shouldn't it be me taking *your* home number and address?' she asked.

He had the grace to grin sheepishly. 'Ah, there you have a point.'

The blonde barmaid put their food in front of them and Tessa began to eat. 'You will excuse me if I get on, won't you?' she said. 'My daughter needs new shoes and I promised to take her into town after school—which means doing some work in my lunch hour.'

Kevin stared at her ringless hand. 'Ah, so you're a one-parent family, then?'

'I'm the divorced mother of a six-year-old daughter,' she told him. 'And just for the record, Kev, I don't think *labels* have any place in our kind of work, do you?'

For a split second he looked taken aback, then the grin she was rapidly becoming familiar with spread over his features. 'I did ask you to tell me about yourself, Tessa. If you choose not to then you can hardly blame me for putting two and two together, now can you?'

Tessa was about to reply when a familiar figure on the far side of the bar caught her attention. Dr Paul Nathan was talking to the landlord. He finished his conversation and began to walk towards the door. But a moment later he caught sight of her. His eyes swiftly took in the table for two in the window, the heads bent over the food, drawn close in conversation, and he made to turn away, but Tessa quickly held up a hand in greeting, beckoning him towards them. Somewhat reluctantly he began to make his way across the crowded bar.

Kevin had taken in the flushed confusion on his companion's face and followed her gaze towards the tall man edging his way towards them.

'Mmm—boyfriend?' he speculated. 'Don't worry, I'll

put things right for you.'

Tessa shot him a furious look. 'No need. It's Dr Nathan, from the Health Centre,' she corrected.

Kevin Donaghue greeted Paul amiably. 'Hi, Dr Nathan.' He offered his hand without getting up. 'Kev Donaghue, your new social worker. Thought I'd take my new colleague out to lunch—get to know her.'

'I see—how do you do.' Paul's eyes were noncommittal as he shook the proffered hand. He took in the casual clothes, the scuffed jeans and anorak. He glanced at the glass of colourless liquid in front of Tessa, then briefly and coolly at her face. 'Well, I'll leave you to it. Enjoy yourselves.'

'That's only mineral water she's drinking,' Kev put in quickly. 'Wouldn't touch a drop of anything else in working hours, I'm sure you'll be glad to know.' He winked broadly at Tessa. 'And I daresay she's dying to ask how *you* come to be in the pub at lunchtime!'

Tessa winced as Paul said: 'A house call, as it happens. I came through the bar to have a word with the landlord. Perhaps I'll see you later.' He nodded to Tessa and turned away abruptly. She watched the back of his dark head as he made his way towards the door and passed through it without a backward glance.

Watching her closely, Kev asked with characteristic frankness: 'Is he married?'

She shook her head.

'Mmm, interesting—wonder why?' he muttered. 'Are you in love with him?'

Tessa's eyes flew open at his audacity. 'I *certainly* . . . it's none of your business!'

He narrowed his eyes at her, sucking in his breath. 'Phew—*that* bad, eh? Well, for what it's worth, my advice is, don't waste your time. He looks a pretty cool customer to me. Anyway, a guy that good-looking should have been snapped up years ago. The fact that he hasn't seems to point to some character defect. I'd be wary if I were you.'

'Do you judge everyone so arbitrarily?' she asked hotly. 'If you ask me, I'd say *that* was a pretty serious character defect—especially for someone in your line of work!' She rose from the table, gathering up her bag and jacket. 'Thanks for the lunch, Mr Donaghue. It was *very* illuminating!'

CHAPTER NINE

TESSA met Beverley from school that afternoon as she had promised. After the new shoes had been chosen there was to be a tour of the shops and tea out as a special treat. As they stood at the bus stop Beverley chattered constantly about the coming treat.

'Mandy says that if you have tea at Fraser's ladies come round in pretty dresses to show you what they look like,' she announced. 'Can we go there, Mummy?'

Tessa was still preoccupied with thoughts of the morning's encounter with Kevin Donaghue. She frowned down at her small daughter. 'Ladies in pretty dresses—what on earth do you mean?'

'Like on television,' Beverley explained patiently. 'They're called muddles.'

Tessa laughed. 'Oh! You mean *models!*'

Beverley shook her head. 'Mandy said they were muddles.' Her puzzled frown disappeared as a car drew into the kerb close by. 'Oh, look! There's Paul.' She waved frantically. 'Paul! Cooee!'

He drew alongside them and wound down the window. 'Hello, young lady. Are you going into town?'

Tessa's heart sank into her shoes, but before she could do anything to prevent her Beverley was saying eagerly: 'Yes. We're going to get me some new shoes—and after that we're going to have tea at Fraser's and see the muddles!'

He reached across and opened the passenger door. 'In that case you'd better jump in. I happen to know there won't be another bus for a quarter of an hour.'

Tessa hesitated. 'Ah, I wouldn't want you to go out of your way for us.'

'I won't be. I'm going into town myself,' he told her abruptly.

Unable to refuse without appearing rude, Tessa reluctantly gave in. Making sure that Beverley was safely strapped in, she fastened her own seat-belt, glancing at Paul as she did so. 'It's very good of you to give us a lift.'

'Not at all.' He glanced at her, one eyebrow raised. 'May one enquire what *muddles* it is you're off to see?' he asked quietly.

'Beverley means models,' she explained. 'A friend at school has told her they have fashion shows in the restaurant at Fraser's.'

He laughed. 'Oh, I see.' After a moment he glanced at her. 'You seemed to be getting along well with your new colleague at lunchtime.'

'Well, he's certainly very enthusiastic,' she said noncommittally.

Paul didn't pursue the subject further. Tessa glanced at him, but his expression revealed nothing. 'Were you visiting Mrs Brown at the Fox and Grapes?' she asked by way of changing the subject. 'I heard she was poorly.'

He nodded. 'Her asthma again. It's the fourth attack this month.'

'What a pity. It must make things hard for her husband. There's a lot to do in a pub,' Tessa said.

Paul shrugged. 'Between ourselves I think the woman is rather a hypochondriac. If it isn't her chest it's something else. Hardly a week goes by that she isn't at the Centre with some new ailment.' He shook his head. 'Then there's her smoking, of course. As I told her, it's hardly conducive to a healthy chest.'

Tessa was silent, remembering the peaky, nervous-looking Mrs Brown with her wheezy cough. She would have hazarded a guess that it would take more than giving up cigarettes to improve the woman's condition. It was all too easy for those who had never been ill to criticise. Although Paul was highly thought of as a doctor, she suspected that there were times when he could seem unapproachable and unsympathetic. But she kept her thoughts to herself as they drove on to the forecourt of the multi-storey car park in the town centre.

Paul stopped to let them out and Tessa thanked him for the lift, but before he could drive away Beverley piped up in her clear childish voice:

'Would *you* like to have tea with us and see the muddles at Fraser's, Paul?'

Tessa shot her a reproving look. 'Dr Nathan is busy, Beverley,' she said firmly. 'He won't have time for that.'

'Oh, I think I will.'

His tone was firm and Tessa looked at him in surprise. 'Oh, but there's really no need,' she said hurriedly. 'Beverley didn't mean . . .'

'It's rather nice to be invited to tea by a lady,' he said, smiling at Beverley. 'Thank you very much. I'm sure I'll be gasping for a cup by the time I've finished my errands. Shall we say five o'clock in Fraser's, then?'

Beverley nodded eagerly and before Tessa could say another word Paul had wound up the car window and was driving off to find a parking space. She looked unhappily down at her small daughter.

'I wish you wouldn't do that, Beverley,' she said reprovingly. 'I've told you about it before.'

Beverley smiled up at her unrepentantly. 'Paul likes me,' she said simply. 'And he hasn't got anyone to have tea with, has he?'

'He may have for all we know. And if he hasn't he

probably likes it that way,' Tessa told her. 'You should
always give people a chance to say no if they want to.'

Beverley looked puzzled. 'But he didn't *want* to say no,
Mummy. I know he didn't!'

Tessa sighed exasperatedly and took the child's hand.
'Oh, come on. We'd better go and get those shoes before the
shops close.'

At five o'clock they mounted the escalator in Fraser's
department store and made the ascent to the restaurant
on the top floor, Beverley chattering excitedly all the
time about her new shoes. They had finally arrived at a
compromise between the red ankle-strapped ballet shoes
Beverley fancied and the sensible brown school brogues
Tessa intended her to have. Button-bars in a subdued
shade of cherry had been settled on in the end, and
Beverley proudly clutched the box containing them under
one arm.

As their heads drew level with the restaurant floor
Beverley's eyes immediately began raking the room
for Paul, and when she caught sight of him waiting
at a table for three by the window she said excitedly:

'There he is! There's Paul!' And it was only Tessa's
hand on her shoulder that prevented her from running to
meet him.

Much to Beverley's disappointment there was no fashion
show that afternoon, so Paul insisted on ordering her
an extra large ice-cream sundae to make up. But when
the waitress brought the bill Tessa picked it up quickly.

'You must let me pay,' she told him firmly. 'After all,
Beverley did invite you.'

'All right, as long as you let me pay for Beverley's
ice-cream,' he conceded gravely. 'That was my treat.'

Once Beverley had stopped chattering about her new
shoes and started to apply herself to her ice-cream, silence

fell. Paul glanced at Tessa and said quietly:

'There's something I want to talk to you about. If you're free this evening perhaps we could have dinner.'

She looked up at him in surprise. 'What is it? Can't you tell me now?'

He glanced at Beverley and smiled ruefully. 'Hardly.'

'Tonight is difficult,' she said, her eyes avoiding his. 'It's my FSG surgery.'

'Then perhaps we could have a quiet drink afterwards.' He was obviously not to be put off. 'I'll pick you at the Centre around eight?'

To Tessa it sounded more like a command than an invitation and she felt resentment niggling at her. It would serve him right if she told him to get lost! 'Well, if it's important . . .' she said. 'And if it won't take too long . . .'

It was a very long time since Tessa had had a date with a man—though she wasn't at all sure that the arrangement she had made with Paul could be regarded as a date. Getting ready to go to the Centre that evening she found it difficult to decide what to wear. For her FSG surgery she liked to dress informally—on the other hand, if she was going out afterwards . . . She put on a pretty green silk dress, then impatiently pulled it off again. Paul's invitation hadn't sounded particularly lighthearted. She didn't want to arrive in something unsuitable. Finally she chose a businesslike navy suit teamed with a white silk shirt.

Downstairs in the hall Nell urged her not to hurry home, assuring her that Beverley would be fine. 'Just relax and enjoy yourself,' she said with a smile. 'I'm glad to see that you're taking my advice.'

Tessa pulled a face. 'I don't know that I'm doing that exactly. Paul Nathan said he wanted to talk to me about something. It sounded almost ominous—hardly a social occasion.'

'Is that why you're dressed like a schoolmarm?' Nell asked.

Tessa looked down at herself. 'Oh, is that how I look?'

'Oh, you look very smart, don't get me wrong,' Nell assured her. 'Just a little on the defensive, if you see what I mean.'

But Tessa had little opportunity to mull over this last remark. The surgery was busy that evening. Most of her 'patients' were routine, mothers worrying over various problems with their children, but as Tessa saw the last patient out she found one more waiting for her. Mrs Brown from the Fox and Grapes sat in a corner of the waiting room nervously puffing at a cigarette in spite of the 'No Smoking' notice conspicuously displayed on the opposite wall. The woman looked ill and, knowing that she had been visited by Paul only that morning, Tessa questioned the wisdom of her being out of bed. Smiling, she invited the woman into her room and when she was seated, asked gently:

'What can I do for you?'

'I had to talk to someone. I can't go on much longer.' Sylvia Brown began to cough and Tessa handed her an ashtray for the offending cigarette. Getting up, she poured her a glass of water. 'Here, drink this.' She pressed the glass into the woman's trembling hand. 'And take your time. There's no hurry.'

After a moment or two Sylvia Brown composed herself once more. 'It's Bob,' she said bleakly. 'Everyone thinks we're the ideal couple.' She gave a bitter little laugh. 'Little do they know?'

'What don't they know?' Tessa asked gently.

'Oh, he's always joking,' Sylvia went on. 'He's kind-hearted and generous. I daresay a lot of women even envy me.' She fumbled in her bag for another cigarette. 'He's good-looking and smart too; quite the perfect husband, in fact.' She stuffed the crumpled cigarette packet back and pulled out a hanky instead. 'I expect you've guessed,' she muttered, dabbing at her nose and eyes. 'It's other women. He just can't resist them. He's been like it ever since we were first married. Sometimes I think it's almost a kind of disease with him.' The words poured out. 'He denies it, of course, when I tax him with it. But I'm not blind—I see the way he looks at them. She shrugged her thin shoulders. 'The rows and the strain are making me ill. My chest is bad nearly all the time now. I just don't think I can cope with much more of it.'

'Do you *want* to cope with it?' Tessa asked. 'I think that's what you must ask yourself first. Is your marriage worth fighting for?'

The look in Sylvia Brown's eyes held the answer even before she gave it. 'I still love him, if that's what you mean,' she said unhappily. 'I expect you're wondering why. I don't know the answer to that. I must be a fool, I suppose.'

'Of course you're not a fool,' Tessa told her. 'Look, I'm always here to lend an ear to your problems, but I think you should have expect advice on this one. I suggest you go along and talk to the local Marriage Guidance Counsellor.'

The other woman shook her head. 'Bob would never agree to go to one of those,' she said. 'He can't see that we have a problem and anyway, he'd hate me telling other people about it. If he knew I was here talking to you he'd be furious.'

Tessa was firm. 'If you can't get your husband to go with you then go alone. I think you'll find it's worth making the effort. You owe it to yourself, Mrs Brown. But the first thing is to get yourself fit again. Go home and rest—take your medicine. It's important not to neglect yourself. Then the moment you feel better, ring and make yourself an appointment.' She took a card out of her drawer and passed it over to the woman. 'The address and a telephone number to ring are here. Make up your mind to do something positive about your problem, Mrs Brown. Often just making a firm decision can help enormously.'

The woman took the card, looked at it for a moment, then slipped it into her handbag. She began to look more relaxed. 'I thought you'd tell me to give up smoking—go to a health farm and get myself glammed up, make myself more attractive,' she said, selfconsciously touching her dishevelled hair.

Tessa smiled. 'All those things have strong possibilities, Mrs Brown,' she said. 'And the fact that you've thought of them shows that you haven't given up hope. But you won't feel strong enough to tackle any of them until you attend to your health. It's a question of priorities; health first, advice next, then action.' She smiled. 'And in the meantime, if you want someone to talk to I'm always here on Wednesday evenings.'

Seeing Sylvia Brown out, Tessa paused for a moment to think of Paul's remarks that afternoon. He had accused the woman of being a hypocondriac. It was all too easy to write off the too-frequent patient in this way. Recurring illnesses were often a cry for help.

Paul was waiting with the Stag on the Health Centre car park when Tessa came out ten minutes later. As she got in and fastened her seat-belt he asked:

'Are you hungry?'

She shook her head. 'Not specially. I ate with Beverley before surgery.' She glanced at him. 'But if you want to eat . . .'

'I can always make myself something later,' he said dismissively. 'We'll drive out for a drink. I know a little place in the next village.'

Glancing at his profile as they drove, Tessa found herself wondering what it was he wanted to say. She would rather have got it over with here and now and dispensed with the polite ritual. She sighed and settled back in her seat, deciding that she would have to wait.

The 'little place' Paul had mentioned turned out to be a tiny thatched inn on the edge of a village about five miles from Laughton Mere. In the small, cosy lounge they found a quiet corner. As Paul was at the bar getting drinks Tessa wondered whether she should tell him about Sylvia Brown. The woman was his patient after all, and he had obviously misjudged her. She decided to wait and see how things progressed.

He wore casual slacks and a sweater, in sharp contrast to her own formal suit, and he looked very relaxed as he sat down opposite her. Crossing one long leg over the other he raised his glass to his lips. Something about the gesture irritated Tessa, grating her already thin patience raw.

'What was it you wanted to talk to me about, Paul?' she asked crisply. 'I must say it sounded rather ominous.'

He looked up at her with mild surprise. 'It's nothing much. I'm sorry if it sounded ominous. That wasn't the intention.'

'Well?' she challenged, meeting his eyes. 'Are you going to end the suspense—put me out of my misery?'

His eyebrows rose. 'For heaven's sake, Tessa! I only wanted a quiet chat.'

'So why aren't we having it?' She was really annoyed now. Leaning towards him, she said angrily, 'Ever since we went to Wellesea that Sunday you've been avoiding me. Well, I'd like you to know that you needn't worry. I'm not a mushy-hearted romantic like Alison Moss, and I'm not a predatory meal-ticket hunter either!'

He frowned, putting his glass down on the table with a thump. 'Would you mind telling me what you're talking about?' he demanded.

'You *know* perfectly well,' Tessa insisted. 'Look, I know all about the unfortunate Alison Moss and her hopeless passion for you. It must have been very awkward for you, but you needn't be afraid you've got another of her kind on your hands, because as far as I'm concerned—in spite of the impression you probably got—there is *no* place in my life for a man—*any man!*' She hadn't paused to take breath during this last speech and now she sank back in her chair, flushed and slightly breathless. Picking up her glass, she drained it at one gulp, almost choking in the process.

She was still spluttering when Paul said: 'Well, I won't pretend to know what brought that on, but I can assure you that I intend to find out.' He drained his own glass. 'As you've obviously finished your drink, I think we'd better go. This is hardly the place for what I have in mind.'

Without waiting for a reaction from her he got up and walked towards the door. Slightly chastened, Tessa followed. Had she gone too far? She really shouldn't have mentioned Alison, she supposed. Oh well, it was too late now.

As he held the door open for her she passed through it with a defiant look in his direction. He needn't think he could intimidate her with those glowering eyes!

In the car she glanced at him, but he neither returned her look nor spoke. 'Would you mind telling me where we're going?' she asked as he started the car.

He threw her the briefest of glances. 'Wait and see!'

He drove very expertly and very fast through the country lanes and in what seemed mere minutes they were back in Laughton Mere. The Stag slipped silently through the village and finally ran into an open garage, where he stopped the car and unfastened his seat-belt. He turned to Tessa.

'Shall we go inside?'

She looked around. 'Where are we?'

Reaching across, Paul opened the door for her. 'My place,' he told her briefly.

Getting out, she saw that they were outside a smallish, two-storey block of flats on the fringe of the newer part of the village. Paul took her arm and steered her in through the front door and up the stairs to the first floor. Taking out his key, he opened the door and she found herself in a large studio flat with a window overlooking the church tower and the thatched roofs of the old village. But her mind was not on the view at that moment. He held out his hand.

'Give me your coat.'

Tessa's eyes widened as she turned to him. 'Why? Why are we here?'

He was standing two feet away and he looked down at her with a wry expression. 'I don't have designs on your honour, if that's what's worrying you,' he said dryly.

She took off her jacket and handed it to him. 'I merely asked . . .'

'I want to know exactly what brought on the sudden outburst back there,' he said. 'What was all that about "meal-ticket hunting", for instance? And just what is this *impression* I'm supposed to have gained?'

He was obviously very angry, and on second thoughts she had gone over the top a bit. She drew a deep breath. 'Perhaps I—owe you an apology—maybe I got things wrong . . .'

'*Oh no!* You don't get out of it as easily as that.' He took a step towards her and grasped her arm, nodding towards the chairs on the far side of the room. 'I suggest we sit down, then you can explain in comfort.'

Tessa swallowed hard, fervently wishing she had never agreed to accept his invitation. She could have been at home at this moment, relaxing with Nell over a glass of wine; instead, she found herself firmly steered towards the large leather chesterfield on the other side of the room and pressed down on to it. Paul seated himself in a chair opposite, fixing her with eyes that seemed to bore, laser-like, through to her very brain. When she didn't begin he prompted:

'I suspect that all this is because of what Beverley said that evening—coupled with the fact that I kissed you,' he said with brutal frankness. 'Am I right?'

She could do nothing to prevent the hot, tell-tale colour from searing her face. There was no need to reply. He must surely see that he had hit the nail squarely on the head. Forcing herself to meet his eyes, she said: 'I was afraid you might think . . . I realise now that it was an impulse . . . and I didn't want you to think that I . . .' She gave up. What was the use of trying to tell him that the kiss had meant as little to her as it had to him when with every stumbling word she was saying precisely the opposite!

'Who told you about Alison?' he asked quietly, diverting her thoughts abruptly.

Tessa winced. 'Oh, can't we forget I mentioned that?'

Paul shook his head. 'I'm afraid not.' Getting up, he went to the window, turning his back on her.

'Rosemary warned—told me—in strictest confidence,' she said with difficulty. 'She felt I should know because—in case . . .'

'She wanted you to know that I was a man with very little heart,' he said, turning sharply to look at her. 'A man without feelings. Is that it?'

'Oh *no!*' Tessa sprang to her feet. 'Rosemary thinks very highly of you, both as a doctor and a person. You must surely know that. She simply explained to me why Alison left, that was all.' She walked across to join him at the window. 'Look, Paul—since the break-up of my marriage

I haven't wanted another relationship. Some men seem to think that a divorced woman . . .' She bit her lip. 'Obviously the business with Alison embarrassed you. I just wanted you to know that it won't happen again—not with me—in spite of what Beverley said.'

Suddenly Paul's face relaxed and he laughed. 'We're back to Beverley again! That little lady has a lot to answer for. But I thought we'd sorted that one out. I told you not to worry.'

She shook her head. 'It's not as easy as that.'

For a moment he stood looking down at her, then he said: 'All right, so you've explained. Now I'd like to explain something to you. Rosemary probably told you that Alison was in love with me. Everyone knew it—*I* knew it. But I couldn't return her love and there was nothing I could do about it.' He shook his head. 'I wonder if you have any idea how much of a prize pig that made me feel? I even began to wonder if there was something wrong with me; if I really *was* the heartless brute everyone thought me.'

'Oh, I'm sure they didn't . . .' Tessa began to protest, but he went on:

'All my life I've been self-reliant, you see. I learned never to count on another person for anything. My parents deliberately brought me up to be that way from a very early age, and it's too late to change now. Alison made me begin to wonder if my independence had made me into some kind of automaton, incapable of any kind of emotion at all.' He shook his head. 'If she hadn't left when she did I would have gone myself. I had it all planned—to one of the Third World countries to offer what skills I have there.' He lifted his shoulders helplessly. 'To compensate, I suppose you could call it.'

Tessa's heart contracted as she looked up at him. 'Didn't you talk to anyone about how you felt?' she whispered.

He sighed. 'Haven't I just told you about my ingrained

independence?'

'Rosemary and John would have understood,' she said gently. 'They're such kind people.'

Paul looked down at her with a wry smile. 'I suspect you're not much better than I am at opening your heart.' He dropped his hands on her shoulders and gently drew her towards him. 'It might surprise you to learn that you're the first person I can remember confiding in for a very long time.'

Tessa stood very still, acutely conscious of the warmth of his hands on her shoulders through the thin material of her shirt. 'I'm sorry for the things I said,' she whispered. 'I just wanted to get things straight between us. I should have realised that I'm not the only one with problems.'

'Would it surprise you to learn that you've solved one problem for me, Tessa?' he said quietly. 'Would it send you running for cover to know that you've proved to me that I *can* feel something for another human being?'

She looked up at him, searching her mind for a suitable reply and finding none.

'I've grown very fond of Beverley and you,' he told her. 'I find myself looking forward to seeing you each day. Beverley makes me laugh. She makes me remember my own childhood; makes me feel protective.' His hands on her shoulders tightened. 'And, Tessa, when I kissed you that evening it wasn't an impulse—it was something I'd been wanting to do all day; something I found I could no longer resist. Can you believe that?'

She looked up at him and saw that he meant what he said. Somehow, without her knowing quite how, her arms slipped around his waist. She raised her face and when his lips met hers she closed her eyes and relaxed in his a ms, giving herself up to his kiss. It was some time before either of them spoke. For Tessa, it was enough just to stand there in the circle of Paul's arms, enjoying a closeness and warmth she had tried so hard to shut out of her life for ever. At that moment the complicated obstacle race that was her future simply did not exist.

After a while Paul moved. Rubbing his cheek against hers, he asked: 'Would you like a drink—something to eat?'

She sighed. 'I really should be getting home.'

He held her a little away from him, looking down into her eyes. 'I think you know that I don't want you to go, Tessa,' he said huskily. 'I appreciate how you feel—about being self-sufficient, avoiding the kind of relationship that would complicate your life and Beverley's. I think you understand a little more about my nature too. But it's perfectly possible to enjoy a relationship where both partners knew the score and would respect each other's feelings, isn't it?'

Tessa swallowed hard. 'Yes, I suppose it is,' she whispered.

Paul drew her closer. 'Well——?' His eyes searched hers for a moment, but when his lips closed over hers his kiss was harder and more assertive than before. Tessa felt her heartbeat quicken in eager response. As his arms tightened around her she reached up to wind her arms around his neck, her fingers sliding into the crisp thickness of his hair as she drew his head down to hers. He kissed her again, then bent his head to press his lips into the hollow of her throat, his arms pressing her still closer.

'You'll stay, then? Say you will, Tessa. I promise I won't let you regret it.'

She hid her face against his shoulder. 'Of course I'll stay,' she told him breathlessly. 'If that's what you really want.'

CHAPTER TEN

WHEN TESSA woke the sky was beginning to lighten. Through the window she could just see the top of the church tower, its grey stone turned to pure silver by the soft, pearly light. For a moment she lay very still, letting the magnitude of the step she had taken sink in. She had two choices; what had happened between herself and Paul could be regarded as a monumental change of course, or a pleasant, casual interlude—all depending on her attitude. But even while the thought was going through her head she knew that last night could never, in her mind, be regarded as casual. Somehow permissiveness had never been her scene. Regret settled over her like a fat grey rain cloud. What had she let herself in for? Had Paul seen her attitude as the perfect excuse for a casual affair? Worse—had she herself given him the impression that was what she was looking for?

She turned her head on the pillow, forcing herself to look at his sleeping face beside her. He looked so peaceful, so relaxed and carefree in repose, and she felt a sudden stab of resentment. A no-risk affair described what she had agreed to. But Tessa knew that for her the seeds of pain had already been planted. She closed her eyes, remembering last night in spite of her efforts to shut it out. She bit hard on her lip as she recalled her eager response to his caresses, the shameful betrayal of her body, hungry with a longing she thought she had suppressed. Paul's lean, hard body had reawakened her sexuality like a match held to a fuse, had drawn from her an answering fire she thought she had quenched for ever. She had

126

been so confident when she had agreed that they were adult enough to enjoy an emotion-free relationship. But now she realised that if it were allowed to continue it would be nothing but a cheap affair, an empty sham.

Tessa sighed. Sadly, last night had changed nothing. For her it must be all or nothing—and since it could not be all . . .

As quietly as she could she crept out of bed and dressed. Once Paul stirred and turned, throwing an arm across the place she had vacated. She stood quite still, holding her breath. But to her relief he didn't wake, and moments later she was letting herself silently out of the flat.

The Old Vicarage was a mere ten minutes' walk away. It was still early. If she were quiet, she told herself, she would be able to creep into the house and up the stairs and no one would be any the wiser. But luck was not with her that morning.

As she turned her key and opened the front door the sound of the radio quietly playing floated out into the hall and a moment later Nell's head came round the kitchen door.

'Oh, hi! It's you.' She wore her old blue dressing gown and her hair hung down her back in its thick glossy braid. In her hand she held the teapot in which she swirled hot water. 'I couldn't sleep, so I got up to made a cuppa.' She grinned. 'What's your excuse?'

Tessa sighed wistfully. 'I could use a cup of tea too.'

'Then come and join me.' Nell looked her up and down pointedly. 'Or do you want to go and take off your glad-rags first?'

With a sigh Tessa went into the kitchen and closed the door. 'I owe you an apology, Nell. I should have rung to tell you I wouldn't be back. It was quite unforgivable. I'm sorry.'

Nell spooned tea into the pot and poured boiling water

on to it. 'I may be wrong, but I have a strong suspicion that forgetting to ring me is the least of your soul-searchings,' she said, eyeing her friend shrewdly.

Tessa coloured. 'Why do you say that?'

'Let's just say that the stars in your eyes have a distinctly tarnished look,' Nell remarked. 'OK, then—either talk about it or tell me to mind my own business,' she concluded bluntly. She poured the tea and pushed a steaming cup across the table towards Tessa. 'In the meantime get yourself outside of that.'

Tessa sat down wearily at the kitchen table, closing her cold hands round the warm cup. 'Paul and I went out for a drink after surgery, as you know,' she said. 'It started badly, with me losing my temper and saying all sorts of things I shouldn't.'

'And it ended with the pair of you in each other's arms. How romantic!' Nell grinned. 'So why the glum face?'

Tessa sighed. 'It wasn't quite as simple as that. We talked—and eventually came to the conclusion that we were both adult enough to have an emotion-free relationship.'

'I see.' Nell took a long and thoughtful drink from her cup. 'But now—looking at things practically, you feel you've been conned?'

Tessa shook her head impatiently. 'I've conned *myself*,' she said. 'I should have known I couldn't handle it.'

'Are you, by any chance, telling me you're in love with him?' Nell asked gently.

Tessa's eyes widened. Hearing Nell say it was a shock. It was something she hadn't faced up to and she didn't want to. 'I'm just saying that I'm hopeless at casual relationships,' she said evasively. 'For me it has to be a commitment, or nothing.'

Nell shrugged. 'So—where do we go from here?'

Tessa finished her tea and took a deep breath. 'I go

upstairs and take a shower,' she said. 'Then I give Beverley her breakfast and take her to school. Then . . .' She looked at Nell. 'Then I go to work, where I see Paul and tell him it was all a big mistake.' She rose from the table. 'One thing—he won't be hurt,' she said. 'All he has to do is to look for someone else with whom to have his *casual relationship!*'

Nell said nothing as she watched Tessa go. Thoughtfully she lifted the teapot and poured herself another cup of tea. 'That's what you think, love,' she said quietly. 'But I wouldn't mind betting it isn't as simple as that for him either!'

Rosemary's last patient that morning required a cervical smear test and Tessa went along to assist. To her surprise she found that the patient was Sylvia Brown from the Fox and Grapes. When the woman had gone and she was preparing the sample for the lab Tessa said:

'Mrs Brown has a number of problems, doesn't she?'

Rose nodded as she checked her bag ready for her morning round. 'Her asthma, you mean?'

Tessa nodded noncommittally.

'Paul is treating her for that,' Rosemary remarked. 'She's registered with him really, but she asked if I would do her test.' She closed her bag and snapped it shut. 'Not surprising, I suppose. A lot of women are reluctant to have an unmarried male doctor attending to their gynaecological needs.'

'Was it a routine test?' Tessa asked.

Rosemary shook her head. 'No, she's been having irregular bleeding for some time. Personally I suspect a polyp, but she's got it into her head that it's something more sinister.' She shook her head. 'Perhaps the test will help to reassure her. In any event, I'd like to refer her to a consultant when the result comes back. It'll have to be handled tactfully, though, she's a very nervy person.'

Tessa said nothing, but the pieces were beginning to fit together for her as far as Mrs Brown was concerned.

When she returned to her own room she found Paul waiting for her. He stood by the window, and at the sight of him she felt her heart plunge. 'Oh—good morning.'

He turned to stare unsmilingly at her. 'What happened?' he asked. 'Why did you leave like that?'

Tessa found her legs suddenly weak and to hide her trembling she walked across to her desk and sat down. She had meant to prepare what she would say when they met, but there hadn't been time. 'I—I'm sorry, Paul. Last night was a mistake,' she said.

There was a pause, then he said: 'Oh, I see—a *mistake.* Just like that?'

She glanced up at him. 'It's my fault. I thought I could handle it—but now I know that I can't.'

He leaned his hands on the desk and bent to look into her face. 'So having made this momentous decision you simply walk out, without any explanation—without even trying to talk it through with me. Didn't you feel you owed me that much?'

'As it was to be a commitment-free relationship there wouldn't have been any point, would there? I'm sorry, Paul, but it . . .' she shook her head, at a loss to find the right words. 'It just *won't do!*'

He straightened up, regarding her thoughtfully for a moment, his eyes dark and enigmatic. 'Come here,' he said at last.

Tessa looked at him uncertainly. 'What for?'

His voice was ragged as he repeated the command: 'Just come here!'

She rose and went unsteadily round the desk to face him. 'What—what is it?'

Paul's hands shot out to grasp her by the shoulders,

almost jerking her off balance. 'Are you telling me that what happened last night wasn't special for you?' he rasped, his eyes searching hers. 'Are you telling me that last night was some kind of experiment that failed, that you didn't . . . ?'

'Don't!' The breath caught in her throat and she closed her eyes. Her dark hair swung from side to side as she shook her head. 'I don't want to talk about it. I told you, it was a mistake!'

'And is this a mistake too?' His mouth crushed down on hers, dashing the breath from her body as he strained her to him. It took every ounce of her self-control not to give up and melt into his embrace. It would have been easy to cast caution to the winds and forget the firm resolve that had taken all her willpower. But she held her body rigidly as she pushed her hands against his chest, forcing him from her.

'Paul, please—you're making it worse for me. Please understand. I just want to forget about last night. It should never have happened.'

The door opened abruptly. 'Tessa, I forgot to mention that there's a practice meeting this evening——*Oh*, I'm so sorry . . .' A red-faced Rosemary stood in the doorway, looking confused. 'I—I'll leave the details with Thelma,' she muttered, backing out.

'It's all right, Rose. I was just going,' Paul said, his eyes still fixed on Tessa's face, 'I'll talk to you later,' he said ominously.

He strode past Rosemary and slammed the door behind him with a resounding bang. The two women stared at each other. Rosemary found her voice first.

'My dear, I'm so sorry. I'd no idea . . .'

'It's all right. What was it you were saying—a practice meeting?' Tessa sat down at her desk again, catching her trembling lip between her teeth.

Rosemary frowned. 'Yes—at seven. Tessa, you look really shaken. Are you all right?'

'Yes, yes, I'm fine.'

'I don't want to pry,' Rosemary said diffidently, 'but if there's anything I can do—or say . . . ?'

'There isn't anything, really.' Tessa looked up, feeling that some explanation was due. 'Paul and I had a slight— misunderstanding. It'll sort itself out.'

'Oh dear, trust me to barge in at the wrong moment,' Rosemary said with a sigh. 'Look, if there's anything I can do to ease the situation let me know.'

'I will.'

When Rosemary had gone Tessa found that she was still trembling. She had been surprised that Paul had been so angry; after all, it was only supposed to be a casual affair. She raised her fingers to touch her lips gingerly. They still stung and tingled from the harshness of his kiss. His words rang out in her head: *I'll talk to you later!* Obviously he wasn't letting the matter drop. Thinking about it, she supposed she did owe him some sort of explanation. But it wasn't going to be easy.

During the day Tessa threw herself wholeheartedly into her work, trying her best not to think about her involvement with Paul, but over a midday snack, shared with Rosemary, another problem raised its head.

'What arrangements have you made for the school holidays?' Rosemary asked. 'Only another week now and they'll be breaking up.'

Tessa stopped eating, her sandwich halfway to her mouth. With all that had happened she hadn't realised the summer break was so near. With Nell's pregnancy advancing into its final stages it wouldn't be fair to expect her to look after Beverley full-time. She voiced this worry to Rosemary, who agreed.

'You must take some time off,' she suggested. 'Get Thelma to let you see the holiday rota. Surely there are a couple of weeks free during the school break?'

'Oh, but that wouldn't be fair,' Tessa protested. But Rosemary shook her head.

'You're entitled to a break. Perhaps you could go and spend some time with your mother.' Her face brightened. 'And why not bring her back with you when you come? She could entertain Beverley while you were at work, and that would take care of another couple of weeks of the holidays.'

The more she thought about it, the more Tessa liked the idea. At the back of her mind was the thought that a couple of weeks away from Laughton Mere would help to cool the situation between herself and Paul. Rosemary rang through to Reception and asked Thelma for the holiday rota, but on inspection they found that the only time available was later in the school holiday period.

Rosemary looked thoughtful. 'Why not invite your mother here right away? She could take Beverley home with her and then you could go up later, spend a week with them both.'

That afternoon Tessa rang her mother, who seemed delighted at the idea of a visit to Laughton Mere.

'I thought you'd never ask!' she remarked wryly. 'Are you going to get a holiday yourself this summer?'

'Not until later,' Tessa told her. 'I wondered if you could take Beverley back with you, then I'll come up for a few days and collect her later.'

Before they rang off a date was arranged for the impending visit. As she put down the receiver Tessa smiled, imagining Beverley's delight when she heard that she would soon be seeing her beloved granny again.

Surgery was just drawing to a close that evening when Kevin Donaghue put his head round the door. 'Hi! Any problems?'

Tessa shook her head. 'Not really. There's a practice meeting in half an hour. I was hoping to get a quick coffee.'

'I know about the meeting,' Kevin said, coming in and perching on a corner of her desk. 'I'm invited to sit in as a prospective member of the staff. I was hoping you'd brief me on a couple of cases so I'd be able to contribute a little.'

'Well . . .' Tessa looked doubtful.

'Look, I *am* a social worker,' he reminded her. 'I do have some experience in human problems. What's the trouble? Is there something shifty-looking about me?'

Tessa flushed. 'Of course there isn't!'

'Then why all the reluctance to share case notes with me?'

'It's just that these people come to me—tell me their problems in confidence,' Tessa said.

Kev lifted his shoulders in an exasperated gesture. 'So what do you think I'm going to do—broadcast the facts in the local paper?' He spread his hands. 'Look, love, they must surely realise that you can't have *all* the answers!' he said. 'You're not God, are you? So why not let me give you—and them—the benefit of my experience?' He leaned across the desk to peer into her eyes. 'Look, if you've got a thing about it you can give them false names if you like, they way they do in the agony columns— you know, Worried Blue-Eyes from Tunbridge Wells.'

Tessa looked at him. She was well aware that he was sending her up, but it seemed she had no choice. If Kevin Donaghue was coming to work at the Centre—and it looked as though he was—she had little option but to let him in on the Family Support Group.

He gave her his disarming grin and reached out to ruffle her hair. 'Come on, get your coat and I'll take you for a drink,' he announced. 'We've just got time before the meeting, and maybe you'll feel more relaxed over a pint.'

She got up and reached for her jacket and handbag. Kevin opened the door and steered her through it, one hand firmly grasping her arm. They had just reached the end of the corridor when Paul's door suddenly opened and he stood facing them. Ignoring Kevin completely, he said.

'Tessa, I was about to come and see you.'

She felt the warm colour creeping up her neck into her cheeks. 'Oh, I—er—we were just . . .'

'Going to the pub,' Kevin completed the sentence for her. 'Why don't you join us?' The social worker grinned cheerily. 'We haven't met properly. It would give us a chance to get to know each other.'

Paul looked irritated. 'I don't think that will be necessary,' he said brusquely without taking his eyes from Tessa's face. 'I really did want to talk, Tessa. It's important.'

She felt panic thicken her throat. 'There really isn't time now,' she muttered. 'Maybe later.' Kevin was tugging at her arm.

'If we're going to have that drink we ought to get going, Tess.'

'Yes—yes, I'm coming.' She allowed herself to be pulled away, but her heart gave a lurch as she saw the look on Paul's face. He really was angry with her, but there was something else in his expression too—bewilderment and, if she hadn't known him better, she would almost have said *hurt*!

'It's just his ego,' she muttered under her breath as Kevin hurried her along. 'No doubt he's used to getting things all his own way when it comes to the opposite sex! He's just like all the rest—he thinks that as a *discarded* woman I should fall into his arms with the utmost gratitude!'

'What did you say?' Kevin asked as they climbed into his battered Citroën.

'Nothing,' Tessa shook her head as she fastened her seat-belt. 'Just thinking aloud.'

He glanced at her as he switched on the ignition. 'What's the matter with Dr Nathan?' he asked. 'He looked to me like a guy with an outsized chip on his shoulder, and I've seen a few of them in my time, so I should know!'

As they sipped their drinks in the bar of the Fox and Grapes, Tessa noticed that Sylvia was absent. Bob, her husband, was a pleasant, jovial-looking man of about forty. He seemed popular with the customers, yet she saw no evidence of the flirting his wife had complained of.

'Penny for them.' Kevin was looking speculatively at her. 'You haven't taken your eyes off the landlord since we came in. What's up, does he short-change?'

She laughed. 'Not as far as I know. I was thinking about something else, that's all.' She looked at him. 'Look, Kev, if I give you the details of a case, will you give me your opinion?'

He groaned and raised his eyes to the ceiling. 'Isn't that just what I've been trying to get you to do?'

She took a deep breath. 'Well, we have a woman in her late thirties, nervous and highly strung—asthmatic. She suspects her husband of promiscuity.'

Kev pulled a face. 'Mmm, not much to go on. So much depends on the two people concerned. Do you think her asthma is psychosomatic—brought on by some deeper cause? Any problems with their sex life?'

Tessa shook her head. 'Those things are not my field, which is why I advised her to try Marriage Guidance.' She took a sip of her drink. 'Something interesting did crop up today, though. It appears she has a gynaecological problem which is worrying her.'

Kev nodded wisely. 'Ah well, I'm not a psychiatrist,

but it seems pretty straightforward. I'd guess that she's probably suffering from feelings of inadequacy—and suppressed guilt; consequently she suspects the husband of losing interest in her and taking his pleasures elsewhere.'

'That's what I thought too. So what would you advise?' Tessa asked.

He shrugged. 'It'll probably sort itself out once the health problems have been solved.'

'That was my advice,' she told him, feeling pleased with herself. 'And at least it looks as though she's doing something positive about putting her health straight.'

'Mind you, it might help to have a word with the husband,' Kevin went on. 'The poor guy probably hasn't a clue what's going through his wife's head. You'd be surprised how many husbands and wives haven't the first clue as to what makes their partner tick, you know.'

'I don't think I would,' Tessa said wryly, half to herself. She smiled at him. 'Well, thanks for your opinion. It's reassuring.'

'That's what I'm supposed to be here for.' He looked at her thoughtfully. 'How about having a bite to eat after the meeting?'

She shook her head. 'Sorry. I have a small daughter waiting for me at home. And I was out last night.'

He shrugged. 'OK, we'll take a rain-check, eh?'

Tessa looked at her watch and stood up. 'Yes,' she said. 'A rain-check.'

When they arrived back at the Centre everyone was there except Rosemary. John announced that she was at the District Hospital's GP Unit and they were to start without her. The two remaining seats at the table were between Paul and James. Kevin seated himself next to James and began introducing himself in his customary gregarious manner, and Tessa found herself sliding into the seat next to Paul. She gave him a sidelong glace which he didn't return.

The meeting progressed, John taking the chair. As they worked through the list of items on the agenda Tessa would have liked to have brought up Sylvia Brown's case, but with Rosemary absent she didn't feel able to. After a moment's consideration she decided to shelve the case until the next meeting. John was about to wind up the meeting when the door opened and Rosemary came in, looking flushed and hurried.

'Sorry I'm late,' she said, shrugging off her coat. 'A difficult delivery at the hospital.' She sighed and lowered herself into the seat next to John with obvious relief. Tessa got up to pour her some coffee from the ever-ready filter machine plugged in at a side table, and Rosemary accepted the cup with a grateful nod at Tessa.

'Thanks. I'm ready for this.' She took a deep draught of the hot coffee, then looked round the table. 'This seems a good opportunity to pass on some news; unless I'm very much mistaken we're about to have a problem on our hands.' She put down her cup and took a deep breath. 'The child I've just delivered was Jill Thomas's. You'll remember that she's the surrogate mother for the Slade couple.'

Immediately all attention was riveted on Rosemary.

'Are the mother and baby well?' James asked.

Rosemary nodded. 'As well as can be expected. There's a serious snag, though. The baby, a little girl, was born with a double cleft palate.'

There was a stunned silence, then Kevin, the only non-medical member of the group, said:

'I'm pretty ignorant where these matters are concerned, but isn't there some way of detecting these things nowadays —before birth, I mean?'

'It didn't show up on the routine scan,' Rosemary explained. 'And there was nothing of the kind in Jill's background, so there was no reason to recall her.'

Kevin nodded. 'I see. A cleft palate, though; obviously that's a handicap, but is it all that serious?'

'It can be corrected, but the process is slow,' Rosemary told him. 'It takes years of plastic and dental surgery during the time the child is growing and developing. In the meantime there'll be feeding problems—later speech difficulties; the child will need constant attention and a great deal of love, patience and understanding.'

'Do the Slades know?' Tessa asked.

Rosemary nodded. 'Mary Slade was with Jill all through her labour and delivery. Naturally it was a shock to both women. At this stage it's anyone's guess what the outcome will be.'

The meeting broke up almost immediately. Obviously Rosemary's news had cast a shadow over them. As they were preparing to leave James came up to Tessa.

'Can I have a word?' He drew her to one side and lowered his voice. 'I'd be grateful if you wouldn't mention the Thomas baby's handicap to Nell,' he said. 'No point in worrying her needlessly.'

Tessa nodded. 'Of course I won't mention it, James,' she assured him. 'But the story's bound to get around sooner or later, you know. Bad news always travels fast.'

'I realise that. But maybe by then she'll have had her own baby, so it won't matter.' He patted her arm. 'Anyway, I know I can rely on you to see she isn't unnecessarily worried by the story.'

Tessa smiled to herself. To hear James talk one would think that Nell was a helpless young girl instead of the strong, capable mature woman she actually was. Perhaps James saw a side of her that others didn't, she reflected to herself as she went along to her room to collect her things.

Much to her relief she found Paul's car missing from its customary parking space. It had been an emotionally exhausting day and she had dreaded the possibility of another scene. It was a relief too to find that Kevin had also disappeared. She turned her face gratefully towards home, looking forward to spending a little time with Beverley before she went to sleep.

CHAPTER ELEVEN

AT THE TIME Tessa was walking back to the Old Vicarage Paul was driving his car back to the flat, his thoughts in turmoil. He had always considered himself a good judge of character, so how could he have misjudged her so abysmally? He had thought—really believed Tessa Trentham to be a mature woman who had her life firmly in hand. Instead she had turned out to be disappointingly, and *typically*, feminine! he drove into the garage and switched off the engine. Getting out of the car, he locked it meticulously and slammed down the garage door with rather more force than was necessary.

Upstairs in the flat he stood for a while by the window, looking out over the sleepy, darkening village, desperately trying to unravel the tangle of mixed emotions that tore at him. He was kidding himself if he tried to pretend that there had been no commitment between them last night. It was no casual affair, and if he were completely honest with himself, he had never had any intention that it should be. The last thing he wanted was for Tessa to feel used; he respected her far too much for that. But he had been a hundred per cent sure that what he had suggested was what she wanted. Somehow this time he had got it all wrong—disastrously wrong!

He gave an exasperated sigh, shrugging his shoulders as he turned back into the room to pace restlessly. But *why* had Tessa changed her mind? What reason could there be behind it—and why had she refused to discuss it with him? He had meant to force her into a showdown, but this evening when he had seen her going off with the social

worker, Donaghue, and later in earnest conversation with
James Lamb, his pride had refused to allow him to
approach her again. It seemed she was determined to keep
him at arms' length, deliberately going out of her way to
show him how little she cared for his feelings! *His feelings*.
Paul ran a hand through his hair. What *were* his feelings?
He closed his mind to the turmoil that raged inside it,
remembering, with a stab of pain, his shock on waking this
morning and finding her gone.

Going across to the drinks cabinet, he poured himself a
stiff brandy, tossing it back neat. He stared round the room.
This small flat had always seemed so welcoming, a haven
after a long day, but now suddenly it was cold and
empty—merely a box containing sticks of furniture. It was
as though just by visiting it once, Tessa had taken away its
essential character—somehow left her mark on it so that it
would never again feel complete without her. He could
even imagine that he could detect a lingering trace of her
perfume. Later as he prepared for bed his foot touched
something soft and he bent to pick up a small handkerchief.
In one corner was the initial 'T'. He crushed it in his hand
and threw it aside, suddenly angry. Since she had been
here, since he had held her in his arms, nothing could ever
be quite the same again. He had done the thing he had
sworn never to do—allowed another person into his
life—more, into the very heart of him. And the irony of it
was that Tessa neither knew nor cared about the havoc she
had caused.

It was the following Tuesday evening during the FSG
group session that Mrs Saunders turned up. She sat silently
through the first half of the evening, not joining in and
looking nervous and uncomfortable. Tessa kept watching
her out of the corner of her eye, and during the break she
took her coffee across to where the woman sat, a little

apart from the others.

'You're looking upset, Mrs Saunders. Can I help? Is it Sally?' she asked.

The woman nodded, her eyes filling with tears. 'Our lives haven't been the same since she traced Christine,' she said brokenly.

'Sally's natural mother? She did manage to contact her, then?' Tessa laid a hand on the other woman's arm. 'Do you want to talk about it?'

Mrs Saunders glanced round the room. 'I meant to bring it up with the group,' she admitted, 'to see if anyone else had had a similar problem, but I couldn't bring myself to talk about it.' She looked at Tessa, tears trembling on her eyelashes. 'Since Sally met Christine again it's as though she's disowned us, Mrs Trentham,' she said, her voice thick with desperation. 'It's almost as though she resents—no, actually *hates* us.' She opened her handbag and took out a handkerchief. 'Christine is still very young, you see. She's pretty and vivacious and Sally finds her great fun to be with. She wants to be like her.'

'Are they seeing a lot of each other?' Tessa asked.

'They meet at least twice a week,' Mrs Saunders told her. She shook her head. 'But I don't want you to get the idea that this is a bad attack of jealousy on our part. We wouldn't mind any of it if—well, if Christine were the type of person we'd like Sally to mix with.'

'But she isn't?'

Mrs Saunders sighed. Giving her nose a final blow and putting the handkerchief away, she looked Tessa squarely in the eye. 'There's only one word for her, Mrs Trentham,' she said, 'and that's *common*. She's been married twice since she had Sally at sixteen. Neither of the marriages worked out, and now she seems to hang around with all sorts of unsavoury characters, haunting the pubs and discos—places like that. We're desperately afraid that

Sally will get into something terrible and ruin her life. Already her school work is suffering, and now that the holidays are coming up and she'll have more time . . .' She stopped speaking as her voice broke again. 'Oh, Mrs Trentham, is there *anything* you can do?' she pleaded. 'We're at our wits' end!'

'Do you think you could get Sally to come and see me?' Tessa asked.

The other woman shook her head. 'She won't listen to anything we say any more. She thinks we're a pair of old fuddy-duddies bent on spoiling her fun. But if you were to contact *her* . . .' She looked hopefully at Tessa.

'Well . . .' Tessa hesitated, 'that isn't what the Family Support Group is all about, you know. For me to come to Sally might seem like interference.'

'Just this once—oh, *please!*' Mrs Saunders looked so desperate and imploring that Tessa relented a little. 'Well, maybe if I were to drop in casually some time when she's sure to be around.' Even as she said the words she felt apprehension about the step she was taking. But when she saw the gleam of hope light Mrs Saunders' eyes she added: 'When would be the best time?'

'Well, if you could manage a Saturday morning . . .'

'I'll see what I can do, but I can't really promise any miracles,' Tessa said unhappily. Saturday mornings were precious to her and Beverley, besides the fact that she wasn't at all sure that what Mrs Saunders was asking her to do wasn't unethical.

'We'd appreciate it so much, Mrs Trentham. I know Saturdays are out of working hours and it's an imposition to ask you really, but if you *could* do anything we'd be so grateful . . .'

Mrs Saunders was still chattering nervously as Tessa saw her out. As she sat down at her desk again she sighed wondering what she had let herself in for and if, indeed, she could help at all in this case.

But before she had time to worry herself further about it another problem presented itself. It was after surgery the following morning when the door of her room opened abruptly to admit a glowering Paul.

'Can I have a word?' he asked, his face as dark as thunder.

'Tessa, who had been expecting to see Thelma bringing her a welcome cup of coffee, looked up with dismay. 'Yes—yes, of course.'

'I've just had a furious Bob Brown in my surgery,' he told her. 'I can scarcely believe it, but he tells me that *you* told his wife to go to the Marriage Guidance Council about him.'

Tessa nodded calmly. 'I *advised* her to consult them, yes,' she told him.

'May I enquire why?' he demanded. 'And also why you didn't see fit to inform me about it? After all, she *is* my patient and we *are* supposed to confer on cases.'

In spite of her thumping heart, Tessa kept her voice level as she said: 'Mrs Brown came to me in confidence and in some distress, complaining that her husband was unfaithful. I advised her to seek help of the kind I'm unqualified to give her. Is that wrong?' Her eyes challenged him.

'I still say you should at least have told me about it,' Paul insisted. 'As it was, I had to plead ignorance when the man confronted me this morning. It was hardly likely to inspire confidence in me as his family doctor, was it?'

'I fail to see why, considering that it wasn't you she consulted,' Tessa said. 'As it happens there has been a further development, though, and I did mean to bring up Mrs Brown's case at the last practice meeting,' she told him. 'Naturally, you'll know that she went to Rosemary for a cervical smear test recently. It struck me at the time that Mrs Brown had several problems that may be inter-related and I intended to say so, but as Rosemary wasn't able to be at the meeting . . .'

'Don't you think you may be in danger of allowing your own experience to colour your judgement?' Paul snapped, interrupting her in mid-sentence.

His words were like a slap in the face to her and she stared at him, momentarily stunned. 'That remark was uncalled for,' she told him. 'But from one as insensitive as you are, I suppose it's no more than I might have expected. While we're on the subject, might I remind you that it was you who labelled Mrs Brown as a hypochondriac. I daresay if her husband had heard that remark his confidence in you might have been even further undermined!' She picked up a pile of record cards from her desk and walked towards the door, but Paul remained where he was, standing in her way. She looked up at him, her cheeks flushed. 'Would you mind letting me pass, please? I don't think we have any more to say to each other.'

'I'm sorry,' he said thickly. 'I shouldn't have said that. Tessa we have to talk. Can I see you later this evening—after surgery?'

She shook her head. 'I'm working late. Tonight is my FSG surgery—anyway, Rosemary will be able to tell you more about Sylvia Brown than I . . .'

He gave an explosive sigh. 'Damn it, Tessa, it isn't Sylvia Brown I want to talk about and you know it!'

There was a moment's silence as they stared at each other, then he said:

'Saturday, then? In the evening—dinner?'

'My mother is coming on Saturday,' she told him quietly. 'To stay with Beverley for the first two weeks of the holidays.'

Paul sighed impatiently. 'When, then?'

She frowned, biting her lip. 'Paul, is there really

any point?'

'Yes! I happen to think there is.' His tone was firm.

Tessa swallowed hard. 'Well—maybe I could slip out during the evening. It wouldn't be until after dinner and I could only spare . . .'

'Right, I'll pick you up at about nine o'clock,' he said abruptly and, turning on his heel, he walked quickly out of the room and down the corridor towards his own room.

Tessa watched him go with a sigh. Suddenly life seemed all complications. But a few minutes later Rosemary arrived with news that made her push her own problems momentarily to the back of her mind.

'Mary Slade has just been to see me,' she said, sitting down in the chair opposite Tessa's with her cup of coffee. 'To tell me that she and her husband have come to a decision regarding the Thomas baby.'

Tessa looked up enquiringly. 'And?'

Rosemary sighed. 'It's as I feared. After long and careful consideration they've decided that they can't take the child after all.' She shook her head. 'It's no more than I expected and I suppose it's understandable, up to a point; a handicapped child—and one that isn't their own . . .'

'Oh, but surely it isn't so severe a handicap,' Tessa protested. 'It can be put right eventually, after all.'

'Mary says it wouldn't be fair on the child,' Rosemary said. 'She confided to me that her husband has a horror of handicaps, especially visual ones like this.' She shrugged. 'Personally, I feel it has a lot to do with what their friends will think and say. Like so many people, unfortunately, they see the handicapped child as bearing some kind of stigma.'

'Surely that's a very superficial attitude,' Tessa said.

'Nevertheless, whatever the reason for it, there's no denying that their decision is a practical one,' Rosemary concluded. 'If there's the slightest doubt, the smallest

likelihood that the child will be resented, it's much better
for them to face it now and cancel the arrangement. After
all, that little baby girl deserves all the love and support she
can get.'

'Any chance of Jill Thomas keeping the baby herself?' Tessa asked. But again Rosemary shook her
head.

'Not the remotest. She's adamant that her husband would
never accept it,' she replied. 'She'll be all right. The Slades
will keep to the financial side of the arrangemnt and Jill
doesn't seem emotional about parting with the child. After
all, she'd conditioned herself to the fact that she wouldn't
be keeping it.'

Tessa sighed. 'Poor little scrap. What will happen to
her?'

Rosemary shrugged. 'Care—a foster-home.' She got to
her feet. 'Just another statistic—another unwanted baby like
all the others!' She shook her head angrily. 'Now maybe
you can see why I'm dead against surrogacy.'

Beverley's disappointment that her mother would not be
spending Saturday morning playing with her was slightly
compensated for by the news that they were meeting her
grandmother off the train at Oakmoor station at four o'clock
that afternoon. Tessa and she ate a leisurely breakfast, after
which the little girl went off to find Ben and Zoe in the
garden. On her way out of the house Tessa looked into the
kitchen and found Nell busy peeling vegetables.

'Hi,' said Nell. 'Jim is coming to lunch, so I'm making an
effort for once.'

'Super!' Tessa crossed the big old-fashioned kitchen to
peer over her friend's shoulder. 'What are you having?'

'Roast beef and Yorkshire pud,' Nell told her, 'garden peas and roast potatoes. I've even made an apple
pie.'

'Mmmm, you're making my mouth water,' Tessa told her. 'Lucky Jim! But why today?'

'He's off to spend a few days with his mother in Edinburgh,' Nell explained. 'She's getting on in years and he goes up about twice a year. I thought he'd appreciate a good meal before he left.' She rinsed the potatoes under the tap and put them into the saucepan. 'I suppose you'll know all about Jill Thomas's baby,' she said casually as she tipped cooking salt into the pan.

Tessa nodded. 'Oh—well, yes.'

'No one told me. I had to hear it on the local grapevine,' Nell said. 'I went to see her yesterday,' she went on, glancing at Tessa. 'There was no one else to go. She hasn't any family, you know.'

Tessa wondered if James knew about the visit. 'I didn't know, actually,' she said.

Nell turned and Tessa saw that her face was angry. 'I don't think anyone has given a thought to how that girl is feeling,' she said. 'It's impossible for her to keep the baby herself, and now the Slades have changed their minds what's to happen to the poor little thing? Everyone seems to think Jill has no feelings, but it isn't true! She's riddled with guilt and worrying herself silly.'

'Surrogacy is a very convoluted issue,' Tessa said. 'All these possibilities should be thrashed out before it's embarked on.' She bit her lip, almost forgetting that it wasn't beyond the bounds of possibility that Nell could face a similar situation herself in a few short weeks' time.

The other woman turned back to the stove. 'I know what you're thinking—you don't have to tell me. But in my case it won't happen. Neither Janet nor I would ever allow the child to suffer whatever happened. But then we're in a far more fortunate position than Jill Thomas.'

Tessa's heart was heavy as she made her way to the Saunders' house. The Thomas baby seemed to have cast a

gloom over the whole village. Jill Thomas might be feeling
bad about the child she had given birth to, but Tessa felt
equally sure that the Slades were not going to survive
without their share of guilt and anguish either.

The Saunders lived in a neat semi on the fringe of the old
village. Tessa's ring at the bell was answered by a bright-
faced Sally.

'Mrs Trentham! Hello, did you want to see Mum?' The
girl held the door wide. 'Come in and have a cup of coffee.'

Tessa stepped inside the pleasant sunny hallway.
'Thanks. Actually it was you I wanted to see, Sally. I was
passing, and I suddenly wondered if you'd have any luck
tracing your mother.' She found herself childishly crossing
the fingers of the hand she had in her pocket.

Sally glanced towards the kitchen door and lowered her
voice. 'I did find her, Mrs Trentham,' she said. 'And I'm
glad I did. The trouble is . . .'

At that moment the door opened and Mrs Saunders came
out, wiping her hands on her apron. Her cheeks coloured
with a tell-tale flush when she saw Tessa. 'Mrs Trentham!
What a surprise. Oh, what a pity I have to go out—I have a
hair appointment. But I'm sure Sally will make you a
coffee, won't you, dear?'

The girl looked relieved. 'Yes, that's all right, Mum. Mrs
Trentham and I are going to have a chat.'

The living room looked out on to a pretty garden, and
Sally brought a tray of coffee through to where Tessa sat
waiting. Mrs Saunders had gone out five minutes before
and Sally told Tessa that her father was working. She
poured the coffee and passed Tessa a plate of bis-
cuits.

'Christine heard my request on the local radio station,'
she said. 'She rang me and we arranged to meet. I'm sure
you'd like her, Mrs Trentham. She's still quite young and
very pretty, but she hasn't had much luck in life.'

Tessa sipped her coffee, nodding encouragingly. She wanted to remark that most of us make our own luck, but felt it wiser to make no comment for the moment.

'She's been married,' Sally went on. 'Twice, actually. But both men left her and now she's all on her own again.' The blue eyes looked frankly into Tessa's. 'She wants me to go and live with her, Mrs Trentham,' she confided.

Tessa put down her cup. No wonder the girl's mother was worried! 'Have you told your parents?'

Sally nodded. 'I've told them everything.' She sighed. 'I thought it was best to be honest, but now I wish I hadn't.'

'Do you want to move in with Christine?' Tessa asked.

To her surprise Sally looked shocked. 'Good heavens, no! Christine and I are poles apart. I'd hate to live as she does. I belong here with Mum and Dad and I want to carry on at school and get my 'A' levels. It's just that I feel sort of—well, *responsible* for Christine,' she said. 'I'd like to keep in touch with her, make sure she's not heading for more trouble. But Mum and Dad seem to have changed since I found Christine again. They want me to stop seeing her. They keep saying nasty things about her every time I try to discuss it, then I find myself jumping to her defence and we always end up having a row.'

'Christine did abandon you,' Tessa pointed out gently. 'I expect your mum and dad feel a little resentful about that.'

Sally shook her head. 'She was younger then, afraid and desperate,' she said. 'And anyway, that has nothing to do with it. I feel that in a funny way I'm more grown up than she is. She hasn't been as lucky as me, having a good family life and poeple to love her. I just want to help her, that's all.' She laughed. 'It's almost as though I were *her* mother!'

Tessa came away from the Saunders' house feeling chastened. Sally had more wisdom that her adoptive parents gave her credit for. They were allowing their insecurity to come between them and their adopted daughter, terrified that they might lose her.

Later that afternoon Beverley hopped from one foot to the other, waiting impatiently on platform four at Oakmoor station. She had asked Tessa repeatedly what time it was, and as the hands of the station clock drew up to the hour and the train was announced over the public address system, she could hardly contain her excitement.

'Here it comes!' she shouted at last. 'Here's Granny's train!'

Tessa took her hand and drew her back from the edge of the platform. 'Stand back here with me, then you won't get in the way,' she said.'

'Bet I see her first!' Beverley said excitedly. 'I bet she's wearing her pink hat, the one with the feather.' She gasped as the train ground to a standstill. 'Oh, look, it's stopping!'

As the passengers surged off the train, her eyes searched every face. Then as the crowd thinned Tessa saw her mother coming towards them from the far end of the platform. 'Here's Granny!' She squeezed her daughter's hand and released it. 'Go on, off you go and meet her.'

With a little squeal of delight, Beverley ran to hurl herself into her grandmother's outstretched arms, and when Tessa caught up to them her mother was smiling, her eyes bright.'

'Oh, it's so *lovely* to see you both,' she said, hugging her daughter. 'Letters are all very well and I love being back in Lancashire, but I'll be happier about you both when I've seen for myself where you're living.'

At the Old Vicarage Tessa introduced her mother to Nell: 'Mum, I'd like you to meet my landlady and very good friend Nell Orton,' she said with a smile. 'Nell, this is my mother, Maureen Latimer.'

The two obviously took to each other on sight, but Tessa couldn't help noticing that Nell looked tired.

'Did James enjoy his lunch?' she asked.

Nell pulled a face. 'I think so. We parted on rather a sour note, though. He was annoyed because I was concerning myself with the Thomas baby.' She shook her head. 'He's such an old woman at times!' She smiled apologetically at Tessa's mother. 'Take no notice of me, Maureen. All part of life's rich pattern, as they say.' She looked at Tessa. 'I expect you two have lots to talk about. If you'll excuse me I think I'll have an early night.'

In the taxi on the way home Tessa had warned her mother that she had to go out for a while that evening. She was apologetic, but Maureen waved away her apologies.

'I don't expect you to give up your social life just because I've come to visit,' she said. 'In fact, with me here to keep any eye on Beverley for you and take her home with me for a couple of weeks, I hope you'll take full advantage of that and feel free to go out and enjoy yourself more. From your letters it sounds as though you've been working really hard.'

Tessa didn't attempt to explain that her meeting with Paul was hardly 'social'. She kissed her mother's cheek. 'Thank you, darling, but I'm not having you overdoing things again. I'm hoping to get some time off so that I can come up and spend a few days with you at Haveridge in a few weeks' time.'

As she had expected, Maureen insisted on bathing Beverley and putting her to bed after supper while Tessa got ready for her meeting with Paul. She took a leisurely shower, then looked thoughtfully into her wardrobe. She chose a navy linen dress with a white collar and was just stepping into it when her mother came into the room.

'Oh, Tessa, haven't you anything better than that?' she said.

Tessa looked round in surprise. 'This happens to be a rather expensive dress,' she said.

'Maybe, but so severe for an evening out.' Maureen stepped up to the wardrobe and selected a pretty dress made of soft, swirling silk patterned in shades of apricot and green. 'Wear this one,' she said, holding it out. 'Most men like a woman to look feminine.' She smiled impishly. 'It *is* a man, isn't it? That young doctor—what's his name—Nathan?'

Tessa sighed. She might have known there was no fooling her mother. 'Yes, it's Paul,' she said. 'But it isn't exactly a date, Mum. More of a—discussion.'

Maureen chuckled. 'I see. Well, wear the pretty feminine dress and I guarantee you'll enjoy your *discussion* even more, dear!'

Paul was on time, calling for Tessa dead on the dot of nine o'clock. As her mother was hovering in the hall Tessa felt obliged to introduce them, though it went against the grain to do so. It was quite clear from her mother's sweeping assessment of Paul that she was already sizing him up as a prospective son-in-law.

As he started the car, Tessa asked: 'Where are we going?'

He turned to look at her. 'As I said, I want to talk. I thought, the flat . . .?' she was shaking her head. 'Oh, for heaven's sake, Tessa! What do you think I'm going to do?' he asked exasperatedly.

'Nothing. It's just that I'd rather talk on neutral ground,' she said quietly.

He ran a hand through his hair. 'You make it sound more like a council of war! Look, it's Saturday evening. The pubs will be hopelessly crowded. We wouldn't be able to hear ourselves speak.'

'I don't mind if we just talk here in the car,' she said.

'Though I still can't see that talking is going to achieve anything.'

He didn't reply, but started the car, revving the engine angrily before roaring off. He drove out into the country for some two or three miles, then stopped in a quiet gateway. Switching off the engine, he turned to her. 'Right. Will this do?'

'It's far enough away for me not to be able to get out and walk back, I suppose,' she said.

For a moment they stared at each other, then suddenly something about the situation touched Tessa's sense of the ridiculous and she began to laugh shakily. Paul joined in.

'We're being idiotic. I'm glad you see it too.' He reached out to touch her hand. 'Now will you kindly tell me why you walked out on me that morning?'

Very carefully she withdrew her hand from his, the smile fading from her face. 'It's not your fault, Paul,' she said painfully. 'I thought I could handle an adult relationship of the kind you had in mind. But looking at it in the cold light of day, I realised I couldn't, that was all. I don't want to risk being hurt again. That's the truth of it.'

He was careful to curb an almost irresistible urge to touch her, to take her in his arms. 'I wouldn't have hurt you, Tessa,' he told her softly.

She shook her head impatiently. 'Not intentionally, no, I believe you.' She looked up, meeting his eyes frankly. 'But then you didn't *intend* to hurt Alison Moss, did you?' He was silent and she went on: 'I accept that it would be realistic for both of us to enjoy the kind of affair where emotions don't impinge or disrupt. It's just that I know now that I'm not the kind of person who can cope with that.'

His eyes moved over her face; while he was taking in what she was saying a tiny part of his mind was noticing the sooty shadow her dark lashes made on her cheek, the creaminess of her skin; remembering achingly the warmth of her body in his arms and the sweetness of her lips on his. He drew a deep breath and cleared his throat.

'You told me once that Beverley was your whole life,' he said slowly. 'That all you needed from life was her and your work. That being the case . . .'

'And I think it's better that I stick with that!' A lump thickened her throat as her eyes slid resentfully away from his searching blue gaze. 'I'm not like you, Paul. You don't *need* people. You don't allow them close enough to hurt you. I'm not like that.'

Paul's heart gave a painful lurch as he took in the implication of what she was saying. In a similar situation with Alison he had been filled with horror, guilt and embarrassment. With Tessa it was totally different. It was like having a butterfly on the palm of his hand. If he didn't hold it, it might fly away for ever; yet grasp it, and it would be crushed. Either way he was about to lose it.

'What do you want, Tessa?' he asked.

Filled with a crushing sense of disappointment, Tessa looked down at the hands clasped in her lap. 'To be—left alone, I suppose,' she whispered.

'Are you sure—*quite* sure?'

'Quite sure.' She sighed. 'I think you'd better take me home now.'

They drove in silence, each of them occupied with their own thoughts. Tessa's heart ached with despair. For her it was too late to avoid the hurt. If Paul had said the one thing she had been waiting to hear she would have thrown herself ecstatically into his arms. But he hadn't—obviously couldn't.

Paul's mouth was set in a grim line as he concentrated on the road. Beside him was the only woman who had ever stirred in him the painful emotion he was experiencing now. It was as though his lifelong independence and stoicism had erected a barrier in his mind. He had always congratulated himself on being proof against this kind of wounding—mercifully protected from it. Now he knew he had been hopelessly wrong and it was too late; he had lost her. The one thing he had never learned to do was to prove to a woman that she was important to him. If he'd known how to do that he wouldn't have been driving Tessa home at this moment. She had handed the decision to him—he had at least recognised that. And he had failed to take it.

As they drew up outside the Old Vicarage and he realised that his last chance was slipping away he made one last attempt:

'Tessa—look . . .'

She quickly opened the car door. 'Don't come in, Paul,' she said. 'I can . . .' She stopped speaking as the front door was suddenly thrown open. In the rectangle of light thrown on to the path, she saw her mother hurrying agitatedly towards them. Paul heard Tessa's quick intake of breath.

'Oh, God—Beverley!' She jumped out of the car and ran towards her mother. 'What is it? Has something happened?' Turning, she found that Paul was beside her and felt grateful for his presence. 'What is it, Mum?' she repeated, her hand on her mother's arm.

'Oh, I'm so glad you're back,' Maureen said breathlessly. 'I've been watching for you for the last half hour. It's Nell—Mrs Orton. I think she's having her baby!'

CHAPTER TWELVE

'HAVE YOU called the midwife—Dr Denning?' Paul asked.

Maureen shook her head. 'I tried them, but they're both out. I left messages. I wanted to call an ambulance and get her to hospital, but she wouldn't hear of it.'

Paul glanced at Tessa. 'I'll take a look at her—will you lead the way?'

Nell was lying on her bed, and one look at her told Tessa that all was not as it should be. A glance at Paul's face confirmed that he shared her view. He felt in his pocket and handed Maureen his car keys.

'Will you go and get my case for me, Mrs Latimer? You'll find it in the boot.' He took off his jacket and began to roll up his sleeves. 'I'm going to take a look at you, Nell,' he said, then, turning to Tessa. 'Will you show me where the bathroom is so that I can scrub up?'

When she had pointed out the bathroom to him Tessa came back to sit on the edge of Nell's bed. She took her hand and squeezed it reassuringly. 'Why wouldn't you let Mum get an ambulance for you, Nell?' she asked. 'You don't want to take chances with Janet's baby, do you?'

Nell gritted her teeth as another sharp contraction gripped her. 'I'll be all right,' she said stubbornly. 'I can't understand why this one is taking so long. The others were so quick.'

Tessa pulled a tissue from the box on the bedside table and dabbed the beads of perspiration from Nell's forehead. 'Will you promise to take whatever advice Paul gives you?' she asked. 'It could be some time before Rosemary gets that message. And the baby isn't due for almost another month.

158

It isn't worth taking risks.'

Nell relaxed as the pain subsided again. Leaning back against the pillows, her face white and drawn, she nodded weakly. 'All right—whatever he says.'

'Can I do anything?' Tessa asked. 'Do you want me to ring your sister?'

Nell shook her head. 'You can't. They're on holiday until next Wednesday, touring somewhere in Scotland.' She gave Tessa a small rueful smile. 'This baby has caught us all napping.'

Paul came back into the room. When he had completed his examination he took Tessa's arm and drew her out on to the landing. 'It's a breech presentation,' he told her. 'She's obviously been in labour for hours. She's exhausted and getting nowhere. I think I should get her to into hospital without delay. I think it's a strong case for Caesarean section.' He looked at her. 'Will you go and put her in the picture while I go down and phone through—get them to prepare the theatre?'

Tessa reached out to touch his arm. 'Paul, will you talk to her? She's set her heart on having the baby here at home. She's going to take some convincing.'

But Paul shook his head impatiently. 'Just *tell* her!' he said brusquely. 'For heaven's sake, Tessa, you should know yourself, there's no time for discussion!'

The ambulance arrived promptly and Nell was carried gently downstairs and into it. Tessa's mother touched her arm.

'You go with her,' she urged. 'I'll stay here and look after the children.'

Tessa looked at her. 'Are you sure?'

Maureen nodded. 'A woman needs a friend at a time like this. It seems you're all she'd got apart from her children. You go.'

*   *   *

Tessa had been waiting anxiously in the waiting room of the obstetrics unit for almost an hour when the door opened to admit Rosemary. She looked tired.

'Any news?' she asked. 'I got the message about Nell and I guessed you'd be here.'

'Nothing so far,' Tessa told her. 'Luckily Paul was with me. He examined her and found the foetus in the breech position. With its being three weeks premature too he thought a Ceasar would be wise.'

Rosemary sat down wearily beside her friend. 'All this could have been avoided if she'd only come into the clinic for regular checks,' she complained. She looked at Tessa. 'Is Graham Tangie operating?'

Tessa nodded.

'He was on call, yes. I think Paul is assisting.'

'I daresay he is. He and Graham are old friends.' Rosemary sighed. 'Well, she's in good hands. It's all in the lap of the gods, as they say.' She stood up. 'I'll go along and see if I can find out what's happening. If there's any news I'll come and tell you.' She hitched the strap of her bag on to her shoulder. 'Have you any transport home?'

Tessa shook her head. It was something she hadn't given a thought to.

Rosemary nodded. 'OK, you can have a lift with me.'

But twenty minutes later when the door opened again, Tessa looked up to find Paul and not Rosemary standing in the doorway. She rose to her feet, hardly daring to frame the words: 'How is she?'

'Nell is just fine.' His face was grey with tiredness. 'At least, she will be when she's had some rest.'

'And the baby?' Tessa whispered.

'A six-pound boy.' His features relaxed into a grin. 'And before you ask, he has everything in the right place and lungs like a costermonger!'

'Oh—— Oh, thank God!' Tessa's voice hiccupped slightly as a sob caught at her throat. Then to her dismay she found that helpless tears were trickling down her cheeks. Paul took a step towards her and put his hands on her shoulders.

'Hey, what's all this?' he said gently. 'There's nothing to get upset about.' He pulled her against him and for a moment she was grateful to rest her head against his warm, solid shoulder.

'Take no notice of me. I'm—I'm . . .'

'You're dead tired,' he finished for her. 'Do you know what the time is?' When she shook her head he lifted his wrist and showed her his watch. It was just coming up to one a.m. 'Come on, I'll take you home,' he said, an arm around her shoulders.

'But I said I'd wait for Rosemary. She offered me a lift,' Tessa told him.

He smiled. 'I told her to go on—said I'd take you home.'

In the car as she snapped on her seat-belt Tessa looked at him. 'Thanks, Paul,' she said briefly.

He turned to her, looking surprised. 'For what? For doing my job?'

'For—for being there.' She meant a lot more than that, but she didn't know quite how to interpret her thoughts at that moment. For a second he looked at her, then he turned away, starting the car and edging it out of the hospital car park.

'Nell should be home in a couple of days,' he said. 'These things seem traumatic at the time, but they're soon overcome.'

Tessa leaned back wearily in her seat. Maybe for some, she reflected sadly.

But Nell was not home in a couple of days as Paul had predicted. It was a full week before the gynaecologist was sufficiently satisfied with her condition to discharge her from hospital. Tessa had managed to contact her sister on the following Wednesday evening, and Janet was delighted to hear of the baby's birth. Later she rang Tessa back to say she had been in touch with the hospital and been told that Nell and the baby would be fit to leave hospital on Saturday afternoon. Her voice almost sang with excitement over the line.

Knowing that they had some way to travel, Tessa asked if they would like to stay the night, but Janet declined the offer.

'I think we should get the baby home as soon as possible,' she said. 'Under the circumstances I think it's best, don't you?'

Tessa paused, wondering how Nell was going to feel at parting with the baby so suddenly. 'I suppose you're right,' she said.

'I can't tell you what this baby means to us, Mrs Trentham,' Janet said, her voice trembling. 'But believe me, I'm not just thinking of myself.'

It was early the following week when Kevin Donaghue called in. Tessa told him of the Saunders case, adding that she had been to see Sally on the previous Saturday.

He nodded. 'We've had quite a lot of these cases since the new ruling about adopted children came in,' he told her, 'some of them happy, but many of them disastrous.'

'In this case Sally's adoptive parents really have nothing to worry about,' she told him. 'But they're in danger of spoiling the relationship themselves, through their over-anxiousness. They're so afraid of losing Sally's love. It's Christine who worries me. She sounds to me like one of nature's casualties—a born loser. Is there anything you can do, Kev? Sally feels responsible for her in a strange way, and that kind of responsibility is too big a burden for a girl of sixteen.'

'I suppose I could go and have a chat with her,' Kevin said. 'I could get her address through the DHSS. But it'd have to be off the record.'

'I'd be grateful if you'd try, though,' Tessa said.

'Of course I will.' He pulled out the notebook he always carried and made a hurried note in it. 'Any other worries?' he asked, looking up.

'I don't think so.' Tessa began to get up.

Kevin grinned. 'Good, then you can join me for a bite to eat. It is lunchtime.' He held out his wrist, tapping his watch.'

'Ah . . .' she hesitated, 'I was going to snatch a sandwich here. I have some paperwork to catch up on.'

Kevin slipped the notebook back into his pocket, shaking his head at her. 'Aw, come on. Snatching a sandwich sounds really boring. Do you good to get away from the pong of antiseptic for an hour!'

Laughing, she gave in. 'All right, you win.'

Kevin was in his wittiest mood. He was good company and Tessa enjoyed her lunch with him more than she had expected to. She was still laughing at one of his outrageous jokes when he dropped her off at the Centre on his way back into Oakmoor. She was waving and watching the battered yellow Citroën drive away when a voice from behind startled her.

'I see the male of the species can sometimes make you look happy, then?'

Paul was standing in the doorway watching her. She coloured, the smile fading from her face. 'Kev and I had a quick lunch together,' she said. 'We had a case to discuss . . .' Her colour deepened as she realised to her annoyance that she was trying to justify herself to him.

Paul smiled grimly. 'It's getting to be quite a cosy little

habit, isn't it?'

Tessa glared at him. 'If you call *twice* a habit, yes!' She walked past him, but his hand shot out to grab her arm.

'I've been to your room to look for you. I've something to say.'

'What is it?' She pulled her arm away.

'Simply that Rosemary suggests we all three meet before surgery this evening to discuss Sylvia Brown,' he told her calmly. 'The result of her test is through and Rosemary feels we should get together to try to put some kind of history together.' He raised an eyebrow at her. 'Is half past five all right for you?'

Tessa rummaged in her bag for her keys, avoiding his eyes. 'Perfectly—thank you for letting me know.'

When she closed the door of her room she found that she was trembling. Why couldn't she and Paul be friends? He had been so kind, so tender at the hospital on the night when Nell's baby was born. It seemed that they could either be lovers or enemies. No middle course was possible.

The three of them met in the common room that evening at half past five. Rosemary had the result of Sylvia Brown's smear test before her.

'It's as I suspected,' she told them, 'a simple polyp on the cervix.' She looked at Paul. 'I suggest you make her an appointment with Graham Tangie right away. No doubt he'll take her into the short-stay unit and do a D and C. The waiting list isn't long, so she should get if over with quite soon.' Rosemary slipped Sylvia's card back into its manilla envelope. 'I feel in this case the counselling is the most important part. It seems to me that much of Sylvia Brown's trouble is in her mind. First of all, this gynae problem has made sex difficult. That has brought on feelings of guilt and tension which she's tried to eradicate by smoking, which in turn has aggravated her asthma! A vicious circle. So, if you agree, Paul, I'm suggesting that Tessa sees her.'

Paul nodded. 'Of course. Someone should talk to her husband too as she obviously won't talk to him herself.' He shook his head. 'Lack of communication can cause untold misunderstandings and misery.'

Rosemary turned to Tessa. 'Give her a ring and ask her to come in as soon as she can. Assure her that she doesn't have terminal cancer, which is what she's been agonising over. Explain what will happen—you know what to say.'

Tessa glanced at Paul. It was ironic for him of all people to sit there smugly speaking of lack of communication, she reflected. But would he mind her seeing Sylvia? After all, the woman was his patient; he might feel that she and Rosemary were interfering, but his face showed no resentment. 'Right,' she said, I'll get on to her right away. She might even be able to get into the Centre later this evening if I ring her now.'

As the meeting broke up Rosemary touched her arm. 'How is Nell?' she asked. 'I went to see her, but I felt she was putting on a show for my benefit. What did you think?'

'I know what you mean,' Tessa agreed. 'She comes home on Saturday. Her sister is collecting the baby from the hospital and taking him straight home with her.' She shook her head. 'I only hope Nell is as tough as she thinks she is.'

Rosemary looked at her. 'You're looking tired, Tessa. I expect you'll be glad to get away for a week with your mother and Beverley?'

Tessa frowned. 'One thing bothers me, though. Ben and Zoe will be going to stay with a friend of Nell's in Devon the week after next. It was arranged to coincide with the birth. With me away as well, Nell will be all alone.'

Rosemary looked thoughtful. 'Mmm—leave that with

me,' she said. 'I'll think of something. Don't think of cancelling your holiday. You look as though you need it.'

Tessa rang Sylvia Brown, stressing that it was good news she had to impart. She promised she would try to get along to the Centre that evening, and sure enough, when Tessa looked into the waiting room at the end of surgery she found Sylvia waiting there. She explained carefully what the test had shown and what the treatment would involve.

'You'll go into the short stay unit early in the morning and have the operation some time during the morning. Your husband will be able to collect you around teatime. the surgeon will give you a good check-up while you're under the anaesthetic, so your mind will be put at ease once and for all.' She looked at the older woman. 'You have told your husband about this trouble and how much it's been worrying you, haven't you, Sylvia?' she asked.

The other woman looked down at her hands. 'Not really. Well, all that kind of thing—it's woman's talk, isn't it? Men don't want to hear about it.'

'So you've kept it all to yourself?' Sylvia's silence spoke for itself, and Tessa asked: 'The other trouble you told me about—his infidelity; have you ever asked him about that?'

Sylvia shrugged. 'I tried, like you said, but it didn't work. We're not even speaking at the moment. When I asked him to go to the Marriage Guidance Council with me he was furious.'

'He would be if he didn't know all the facts. Look, Sylvia,' Tessa leaned forward, 'it isn't really fair to keep him in the dark, you know. If he knew how sick with worry you've been he'd understand about a lot of other things. I think that many of your suspicions about him might well be unfounded,' she added gently. 'So why don't you talk to him? Tell him all your fears and ask him what he feels?'

Sylvia sighed. 'I know you're right, and I will try.

It's the way I've been brought up, I suppose, to keep my troubles to myself.' She looked up hopefully at Tessa. 'I have given up smoking, though. It wasn't easy, but I haven't had a cigarette for weeks now.'

Tessa smiled. 'Well, that's good. Smoking and general anaesthetics don't go well together at all. But please think about what I've said, Sylvia. Tell your husband. You'll have to tell him why you have to go into hospital, won't you? I'm sure you'll be surprised at his reaction, believe me. Why not go right home and tell him now?'

As she saw Sylvia out she thought about what Paul had said. 'Lack of communication causes untold misunderstandings and misery.' He was right. Sylvia was right too when she said it was in the upbringing. Old habits and inhibitions died hard.

James Lamb collected Nell from the hospital on Saturday afternoon. Tessa went with him, leaving the children excitedly helping her mother to prepare a special celebration tea.

Janet Brooks, Nell's sister, was eagerly waiting for them with her husband. She was a younger, more delicate version of Nell, and there was an air of suppressed excitement about her as she waited for a nurse to arrive with the baby. When he was put into her arms the expression of sheer naked joy that she and her husband exchanged made Tessa look away, feeling that her presence was an intrusion.

In the car on the ride home Nell was silent, but when she arrived her reunion with Ben and Zoe was ecstatic. All through tea two spots of hectic colour burned in her cheeks as she laughed and talked animatedly with them all. James stayed to tea, which was a festive occasion, but Tessa caught him one or twice looking across the table at Nell, a troubled expression in his eyes. Soon after he had left for a dinner appointment, Nell herself announced that she was tired and ready for bed.

On her own way up later Tessa paused, seeing a light still showing under Nell's bedroom door. Should she go in? Perhaps Nell would like to chat before going to sleep. But as she began to open the door she froze, dismayed as the sound of muffled sobs reached her ears. Quietly she closed the door again and went to her own room. This was something no one could help with—a problem Nell was going to have to come to terms with by herself—at least, for the moment.

The following week, as Tessa was looking through the morning post in the office, Thelma mentioned that Paul started his holiday on the coming Saturday.

'Do you happen to know where he's going?' she asked Tessa.

Tessa shook her head. 'I haven't heard him say.'

'When I asked him yesterday he said he was meeting an old friend in London and spending a few days there,' Thelma said.

Tessa unwrapped the latest edition of her favourite nursing magazine and began to leaf through it. 'Oh, that's interesting,' she said.

'Actually, it's a bit *more* than interesting,' Thelma said conspiratorially. 'You see, I've had this postcard from Alison Moss this morning. She was the nurse here before you.'

Tessa glanced up. 'Yes, I know.'

'She works in Kuwait now.' Thelma went on. 'They get lots of leave, you know—because of the heat, I expect. Trips home, all expenses paid. It's really cushy.'

Tessa returned her attention to the magazine.'Really?'

'Well, the interesting thing is this . . .' Thelma waved the postcard under Tessa's nose. 'She says here that she's coming home next week—staying in London where she's meeting an old *boyfriend*!' She pointed excitedly at the words on the card. 'How about *that*?'

Tessa stared at the card, her attention suddenly arrested. 'You mean—you think . . .?'

'Well! It's a bit of a coincidence, isn't it?' Thelma said exultantly. 'She's always had a soft spot for Dr Nathan, you know—well, a lot *more* than a soft spot, I'd say. I always think a family doctor should be married, don't you?' She sighed. 'And they'd make such a lovely couple, her so fair and him so . . .'

Tessa shut her ears to Thelma's excited speculation. Could it be true? For all she knew Paul had been corresponding with Alison since she left. Maybe she would be willing to embark on a non-emotional relationship with him if that was the only way he could be hers! She flicked unseeingly through the pile of post, shocked at the violence of her own reaction—refusing to recognise it as jealousy, an emotion she had never felt in her life before. Paul was despicable if he contemplated raising Alison's hopes again, she told herself. He seemed totally impervious to the feelings of others! At last she gathered up her post with trembling hands and left the office abruptly, unaware that Thelma was still talking. The receptionist stared after her, her flow of chatter interrupted in mid-sentence.

'Well, really!' she muttered. It wasn't like Mrs Trentham to be rude! Could it have been something she'd said?

Halfway down the corridor Tessa bumped into Paul. Feeling as she did at that moment she would have given anything to have avoided him, but he seemed determined to speak.

'Tessa, I was coming to have a word with you.'

'Oh?' She looked pointedly at her watch. 'Will it take long?'

'I just thought you'd like to know that Mrs Brown's appointment has been fixed for a week on Friday,' he told her. 'And her husband looked in last night. She'd told him everything, but he wanted to be reassured that she's going to be all right. It seems they'd had a long talk and things between them are much improved.' He smiled. 'Largely thanks to your chat with her. That's good news, eh?'

She nodded. 'Yes, very.'

'I thought you'd be pleased to hear.' His eyes held hers for a moment, then he said softly: 'We seem to work well as a team when it comes to sorting out other people's problems, don't we, Tessa? It's a pity we can't take some of our own good advice.'

Colouring, Tessa tore her eyes away from his, searching her mind frantically for a change of subject. 'I understand you're off on holiday this Saturday. Perhaps you have something interesting to do!' Too late she heard the iciness in her tone and saw his expression harden. She bit her lip. Why had she chosen his holiday as a subject? Perhaps because it was uppermost in her mind. In an attempt to soften what had sounded like a challenge she added: 'I hope you enjoy yourself.'

'Thank you. I intend to.' Paul's tone was equally icy as he turned on his heel and went into his room, closing the door on her dismayed face.

When Tessa reached her own room and closed the door behind her she found that she was trembling. Sitting down wearily at her desk, she felt as though she had the troubles of the world resting on her shoulders, and she thought longingly of the cosy little retirement cottage her mother had bought in their own native Lancashire. It would be good to escape for a week—away from the Health Centre; away from work—away from Paul?

CHAPTER THIRTEEN

NELL went with Tessa on Saturday afternoon to see Maureen and Beverley off at the station. When they returned to the Old Vicarage the house seemed silent and empty. The atmosphere seemed to hit Nell the moment she opened the front door and she walked into the kitchen and slumped into a chair, looking utterly dejected.

Tessa crossed to the sink and filled the kettle. 'I think a cup of tea, don't you?' she said brightly. 'I'm parched!'

When Nell didn't respond Tessa went across to put a hand on her friends shoulder. Nell looked up at her with brimming eyes.

'What's the matter with me, Tessa?.' she asked in a small, frightened voice. 'I don't recognise myself. I thought I had this thing under control—all planned out, cut and dried, but look at me. I'm *pathetic*!' The tears overflowed to trickle helplessly down her cheeks.

Tessa sat down in the chair opposite. 'You're not pathetic, Nell,' she said gently. 'You're low because of the premature birth—all the trauma of being rushed into hospital like that. What you did was a wonderful and unselfish thing. You saw Janet's face at the hospital when she first held the baby in her arms. For her that moment was a miracle, a dream come true.'

But Nell was shaking her head. 'Do you think I haven't said all these things to myself over and over?' she said. 'In the middle of the night when I can't sleep and in the daytime too! But my mind just won't seem to work logically any more. The one thought that persists is that I gave my baby away, rejected him.' She swallowed hard and made a

171

great effort to quell the rising emotion. 'Go on, tell me I'm being melodramatic—over—emotional,' she said. 'Why don't you say *I told you so*! I can see it in everyone's eyes, even if they don't say it—especially Rosemary Denning's.'

Tessa covered Nell's trembling hand with her own. 'We all want to help, Nell,' she said quietly. 'No one's gloating, far from it. Rosemary's been worried about you from the first. She seemed to foresee something like this happening.'

The kettle boiled and Nell got up from the table and made the tea. When she turned back to Tessa her features were under control again. 'I've thought about it a lot and I think I've analysed what's wrong with me,' she said. 'A younger woman knows she could have more babies of her own. For me, that was probably my last chance.' She looked at Tessa as she poured two cups of tea. 'My last chance and I threw it away,' she went on. 'Then there are the children too. I explained to Ben and Zoe what I was doing for Janet and what it would mean to us all. I thought they'd understood, but since I came home I've realised that they didn't—not fully. They thought the baby would be staying with us, at least for a while, and they were disappointed.' She raised her cup to her lips, took a long drink and then set it down firmly on the saucer, straightening her back. 'So—I've made up my mind what I'm going to do.'

Tessa looked at Nell, startled by her sudden change of mood. 'What's that, Nell?' she asked. 'What are you going to do?'

But Nell shook her head. 'I'd rather not talk about it yet, not till everything's settled,' she said. 'I wasn't completely sure at first. I was afraid I might still be too emotional to be seeing things straight. But this afternoon, when I walked in through the door and felt the silence hit me like a brick wall, I knew—I made up my mind.'

Tessa didn't press her further, but she was fairly sure

in her own mind what Nell's plan might be, and as she lay in bed that night she thought about it. It was clear to everyone that James Lamb was very fond of Nell. He was lonely too and enjoyed being with the Orton family. In a few short years Ben and Zoe would be off to college, setting out on their own in life. It made sense for two lonely people to team up and enjoy life together. Tessa smiled, hugging the thought to herself as she fell asleep. At least now she wouldn't worry about going away and leaving Nell on her own next week.

Tessa had thought Paul's absence would be a relief, but it wasn't. She missed him more than she would have believed possible. She found herself thinking of him constantly. Had he really gone to meet Alison in London? And would she be willing to settle for the kind of relationship Paul seemed to want? Maybe she would see it as a chance to persuade Paul into marriage. Maybe he would decide to join her in Kuwait—or worse, perhaps they would come back to Laughton Mere together. Time and again she found her thoughts wandering and had to force herself to drag them back to the present.

At home she rang her mother each evening for news of Beverley. It appeared she was enjoying her holiday enormously. A friend was taking her for riding lessons and she was progressing well. It crossed Tessa's mind briefly that Beverely might have wanted to speak to her, but she dismissed the thought. Maybe she was outside playing. The weather was certainly too good to be indoors.

Rosemary had asked Nell if she would help at the Centre, filling in at Reception while they were short-staffed. Tessa guessed that it was the result of their talk about Nell being alone during her absence that had prompted the offer. She seemed happy in the work and had also started putting in a few voluntary hours a week at the hospital—as a kind of 'thank you', she explained. Tessa had noticed that since she had made her mysterious 'decision' Nell seemed much happier. James saw Nell most evenings, either having supper at the Old Vicarage or taking her out.

When Kevin looked in at the Centre the following week he brought the news that he had located and talked to Christine Markham.

'She's as you suspected,' he said, 'A born loser. Attracted repeatedly to the wrong kind of man; a sucker for the hard luck story. In debt, out of work—you name it.'

Tessa sighed. 'So when Sally turned up she must have seemed like a lifeline.'

Kevin nodded. 'Exactly. We've talked, though, and I think I've made her see how important it is to stand on her own feet. I *think* I might have persuaded her to try one of these re-start schemes. I found quite a good one for hotel work where accommodation is provided.' He glanced up at Tessa. 'The only snag is that she'd probably have to go down south to one of the tourist areas.'

Tessa looked up at him, recognising what he was saying. 'Away from Sally? Ah, but would she be willing to do that?'

'She was doubtful at first,' he said. 'But I pointed out that she and Sally could write and telephone each other. I really think it might work, Tess. There isn't a lot wrong with the girl, basically. She's taken a battering from life and she just needs to get on her feet, get her self-esteem back. When she does I think she'll be all right—even by the Saunders' standards!'

Tessa smiled warmly at him. 'Thanks, Kev,' she said. 'I'll see Sally and her parents and tell them what you've said. I know it'll be a relief to them.'

He returned her smile, holding her eyes with his for a moment, then he asked: 'And what about you, Tess?'

'Me?' She looked away, colouring.

'Yes, *you*. You've been looking distinctly peaky lately. Is the FSG getting you down? Are you letting other people's troubles get to you?'

She shook her head. 'Not really. There've been one or two of my own over the past few weeks. I've been worrying a little about—friends.'

'Come out to dinner with me tonight,' he said suddenly.

She looked up. 'Tonight?'

Kevin grinned. 'That's what I said. I happen to know you're not on duty this evening.' He leaned towards her looking meaningly into her eyes. 'And I believe the handsome Dr Nathan is away on holiday.'

Tessa bridled. 'What on earth would he have to do with it?' she asked, a little too sharply.

He laughed, raising his eyebrows at her. 'Ah, what indeed?'

He called for her at eight that evening and drove her into town to a quiet Chinese restaurant in a little street near the Cathedral. As they reached it and Kevin opened the door for her, Tessa looked up at the sign above their heads. She repeated the name and smiled.

'The Garden of Tranquillity. Very apt!'

'I thought so,' Kevin remarked. 'It's true to its name too; quiet, and peaceful, and the food is the best in town.' They'd reached the top of the stairs and he turned to look at her. 'I've just thought—I hope you like Chinese food.' His face wore a look of comic anxiety and she laughed.

'I do, as it happens,' she told him, 'though it's a bit late to ask.'

The conversation was light as they chose their meal but as the food arrived Kevin looked at her enquiringly and asked bluntly: 'Right, so what's up? You can tell your Uncle Kev, you know. I'm practically bomb-proof.'

Tessa picked up her chopsticks. 'Sorry to disappoint you,

but I don't have anything to tell you!'

'You mean it's classified information?' He raised an eyebrow at her. 'Come *on*, Tess. Anyone with half an eye can see you're eating your heart out over something—or could it be some*one*?'

'This sweet and sour pork is delicious,' Tessa said brightly. 'No, Kev, the answer to your question is "no".'

But he persisted. 'The answer to which question? I strongly suspect that the handsome Dr Nathan has something to do with that "little-girl-lost" expression. Am I right?'

Irritated, she laid down her chopsticks and looked at him. 'I can't say I'm mad about your turn of phrase, Kev, and if I'd known I was going to get the third degree I wouldn't have come out with you. Can't we let it rest there?'

'Once bitten, twice shy?' he asked, his head on one side.

It was as though she hadn't spoken, and she signed. 'Didn't you hear what I said?'

He began to eat his food with obvious enjoyment. 'Hey, you're right; this pork *is* good.' He chewed thoughtfully, looking at her. 'Drawing on my wealth of experience, I'd say you'd fallen in love again for the first time since your marriage broke up. And you're terrified of letting it happen and getting hurt again.'

Tessa felt the warm colour suffuse her cheeks. 'If you say one more word about it I'm going to get up and walk out of here!'

Kevin held up his hands in mock surrender. 'OK, you win!' His face grew serious. 'But remember, Tess, I am used to hearing other people's problems. Sometimes it takes an outsider to see things in perspective. So if you want any help or advice . . .'

'Thanks, I'll bear it in mind,' she told him. 'And now, can we just enjoy our food?'

Tessa had been determined to keep her problem to her

self, but the sweet rice wine Kev plied her with relaxed her and loosened her tongue, and on the way home in the dim seclusion of the car she found herself obeying an irresistible urge to talk.

'My trouble is that I can't be *casual*,' she told him suddenly.

He glanced at her. 'How do you mean—casual?'

She frowned, searching for the right words. 'Superficial describes it better. I can't have a complete relationship without feeling committed. Especially when it clearly means nothing to the other person.'

Kevin raised his foot from the accelerator, He knew that if he stopped the car she would probably clam up, but he could always drive home the long way round—and slowly. 'You say it means nothing to—this other person,' he said carefully. 'How do you know that?'

'He said as much,' Tessa told him with a sigh. 'An adult relationship, he called it.'

'You mean he hasn't said he loves you?'

She shook her head sadly.

'Some people find that very difficult, you know, Tess,' he told her. 'And usually those are the ones whose feelings go deepest.' He glanced at her, wondering if they were in fact talking about Paul Nathan and thinking that the man must be out of his tiny mind if he couldn't see what he was missing. 'Have you tried telling him how you feel?' he ventured.

She sighed. 'I've explained that the kind of relationship he wants isn't for me,' she told him. 'He didn't make much comment, so I told him I couldn't see him again.'

'And that's that?' He looked at her unhappy face.

'That, as you say, is that.'

'Except that you still love him?'

'I'll get over it.' Tessa sat up straight in her seat and stared out of the window. 'Anyway, I have a strong suspicion that he's gone back to a previous girlfriend.'

As Kevin drew up outside the Old Vicarage he turned to her. 'I'm sorry you're unhappy, love.' His usually brash voice was sympathetic and gentle and Tessa felt tears pricking at the corners of her eyes.

'That's all right. I'll work it out,' she said, blinking them back. 'Thanks for a lovely meal, Kev—and for listening. I didn't mean to bore you with it.'

'I know.' He covered her hand with his. 'And I wish there was more I could do.' He smiled at her. 'But if you ever want a friendly shoulder just remember where I am, eh?'

Touched, she leaned across and kissed him briefly. 'I'll remember. Thanks again, Kev. Goodnight.'

The rest of the week dragged, but Friday morning surgery was specially busy and Tessa scarcely had time to stop all morning. It was lunchtime when Thelma came into her room waving another postcard.

'From Alison again,' she announced. 'She's had a whale of a time in London, so it seems. And she hints that when she sees me next she'll be wearing a ring!' She held the card to Tessa, who saw that it was a view of the Houses of Parliament. 'She doesn't give his name, maddening girl,' Thelma went on, 'just those few words, but I'll bet you any money it's you-know-who.'

Tessa's heart felt like lead as she made her way home that evening to begin on her packing. So that really was that, she told herself. If Paul would actually stoop so low as to take advantage of a girl who was besotted with him, then she was well rid of him! She tried hard to look forward to her holiday. It was just what she needed, this break. By the time she came back she would have forgotten the heartache Paul Nathan had caused her. Determinedly she closed her mind to the thought of seeing him and working with him again. She would face that when she came to it.

But when she arrived at the Old Vicarage a surprise was

waiting-one that put all thoughts of her holiday completely out of her head. As she walked into the hall Nell was coming down the stairs. Her face wore an excited flush and her eyes were shining.

'Tessa, I've done it!' she said.

'Done what?' Tessa laughed, catching her friend's mood.

'Come and see.' Nell turned and led the way back upstairs. Tessa following, mystified.

Opening her bedroom door, Nell tiptoed in. In the corner by the window a tiny baby slept peacefully in a crib. Tessa stared down at the tiny head with its fuzz of soft dark hair—the little face with its pitifully malformed lip. 'The Thomas baby!' she breathed. So *this* was what Nell had had in mind all the time!

'Her name is Daisy,' Nell said softly. 'I'm fostering her. Maybe later adoption might be possible. She'll be having the first of her many operations in a couple of months' time. She's going to need all the love and mothering she can get, poor little pet. And I've got lots of that going begging.'

There was a lump in Tessa's throat as she turned to look at her friend. 'Oh, Nell', she whispered, hugging her, 'I'm so glad—for you both.'

Tessa gave up trying to read her magazine and settled to watch the scenery change in character as the train travelled north. The gently undulating Midlands gave way to the craggy hills of Derbyshire and then to the wild sweeping panorama of moorland that she loved so much. But her heart failed to respond with its usual lift. Even the thought of a week's holiday failed to cheer her.

She changed trains at Sheffield and finally, at about five o'clock, the local taxi trundled her the last few miles to her mother's cottage in the tiny village of Haveridge. She was still paying the driver when she heard a delighted shout behind her and turned to see Beverley hurtling towards her down the garden path.

The child looked tanned and fit, and Tessa hugged her close, exclaming that she had grown in the two week she had been away. Her mother agreed as they sat in the sunlit living room of Briar Cottage having tea.

'She's certainly enjoyed her holiday.' Maureen peered at her daughter. 'And you look as though you're sadly in need of yours too. Breakfast in bed for you tomorrow morning, my girl. I think you're due for a little spoiling.'

But Tessa wouldn't hear of that kind of spoiling. For the three days that followed she and Beverley went everywhere. Piling into her mother's old car, they picnicked on the moors, took a trip as far as the coast and swam in the chilly Irish Sea and walked on the moors. It was on the fourth day that Tessa asked over breakfast.

'What about all this riding you've been doing? Aren't you going to introduce me to your new horsey friends?'

Granddaughter and grandmother exchanged glances, and Tessa looked from one to the other. 'What's this?' she asked. 'I used to ride quite well when I was at school, you know. You needn't be afraid I'll disgrace you. Anyway, who is this new friend who's been teaching you, Beverley?'

'Paul isn't a *new* friend!' Beverley blurted—then clapped hand over her mouth and looked at her grandmother with rounded eyes. 'Sorry, Granny,' she whispered.

Tessa stared at them incredulously. 'Paul has been *here*!' I take it we're talking about Paul Nathan?'

Maureen nodded. 'That's right, dear,' she said calmly. 'He and I met in the village one morning while I was at Laughton Mere with you. I invited him to tea one day and we had a long chat. I told him he could come and stay here any time he wanted somewhere quiet to go. His own parents are both dead, you know.'

'And he took you up on it last week? Well, of all the

cheek!' Tessa slapped her table napkin down angrily on the table.

Beverley looked at her mother with a trembling lower lip. 'Why are you so cross, Mummy? I thought you liked Paul.'

In her anger Tessa had almost forgotten about Beverley. She took a deep breath and forced herself to smile. 'Of course I do darling. I'm not really cross. Look, run out into the garden and play while Granny and I do the washing up, then we'll think what we're going to do today.'

The moment Beverley had left the room Tessa faced her mother. 'All right, what's it all about, Mum? I think you owe me an explanation.'

Maureen Latimer smiled serenely at her daughter. 'Sit down, Tessa, and have another cup of coffee. There's no need for you to get so steamed up. I am entitled to make friends of my own, aren't I?'

Reluctantly, Tessa sat down again at the table, watching with ill-concealed impatience as her mother poured the coffee.

'As a matter of fact Paul asked my advice,' Maureen confessed. 'He was worried about you—concerned that he'd lost your . . .' She glanced up at her daughter. 'Shall we call it *regard*?' When Tessa was silent she went on: 'He didn't tell me what the situation is between you, but he did make it clear that he would like it to improve.'

'So he wheedled an invitation out of you?' Tessa concluded.

'No, that was my idea,' Maureen said. 'I thought he might enjoy it. He had a friend to see in London, though, so he only stayed for a couple of days.'

Tessa's colour rose as she remembered Thelma's postcards. 'I see.'

'He's a very complex man,' Maureen went on, 'with very firmly held convictions and very deep feelings. He and Beverley obviously adore one another. It was quite touching to see them together.'

Tessa looked up, her eyes narrowing. 'What are you trying to tell me, Mum? I hope you didn't say . . .'

'I didn't say much at all,' Maureen sipped her coffee thoughtfully. 'But I did a lot of listening.'

Tessa fumed. 'He obviously charmed you into thinking he was totally blameless!' she said. 'He didn't happen to mention to you that he hasn't any heart—any *feelings*; that he just wants to take all and give nothing! I bet he didn't tell you who he was meeting in London either!' She stared at her mother. 'Well, did he? Oh, Mum, how could you imagine that after what I went through with Simon I'd fall for a man like Paul Nathan?'

Maureen looked across the table at her daughter, shaking her head sadly. 'You know, dear, you're my daughter and I love you, but there are times when I could cheerfully shake you! For all your skill in handling people and advising them in difficulty you can be remarkably blind when it comes to matters closest to you.' She rose and began to gather the breakfast things on to a tray. 'You know, I often wonder how it is that you've never learned how to listen to your own heart!' She walked into the kitchen, and Tessa knew from the ramrod straightness of her mother's back that she had said all she was going to say on the subject.

She was right. Pauls's name wasn't mentioned again, and during the two days that followed they forgot their difference of opinion and enjoyed the holiday together. But Friday came all too soon, and with it the need to begin preparing for the return journey. Tessa insisted that they must stay at home and make a start, but for once Beverley was difficult.

'I wanted to go to the seaside again,' she said disappointedly. 'It's a lovely sunny day, and we won't get another chance.'

'I've told you, there isn't time,' Tessa said. 'I have some washing and ironing to do and all the packing. I can't do it all this evening.'

'Why don't I take her?' Maureen offered. 'It could be some time before I have the pleasure of my grandaughter's company again. Without us here you'll have all day to get ready for the return journey.'

'Well, are you sure it won't be too tiring for you?' Tessa looked at her mother, then at the upturned, expectant face of her small daughter. 'Oh, all right, then. I'll have a hot meal ready when you get home.'

By lunchtime she had taken in the washing and ironed it, placing it in neat piles on the bed, ready to put into their cases. She looked at her watch—still only twelve. She could have a snack and sit in the garden till it was time to start the dinner.

She showered and changed into a blue cotton dress, untying her hair and brushing it out loosely. But she had only just reached the bottom of the stairs when a ring at the bell startled her. She frowned. Her mother hadn't mentioned that she was expecting anyone. Perhaps it was a neighbour. Glancing at her face in the hall mirror, she opened the door, then drew in her breath with a little gasp of surprise when she found Paul standing there.

'Oh!' She found her heart doing odd things and for a moment she had the strange, unreal feeling that she might be dreaming.

'Can I come in?' He was looking at her gravely and she realised suddenly that she was still staring at him.

'Oh—of course.' She stood back, holding the door for him. Her mind was racing ahead. What was she going to say to him? What did he want? Was she perhaps supposed to know he was coming? She wouldn't put it past her mother . . .

'I'm sorry to drop in unexpectedly like this,' he said.

'It's just that I was up this way and I thought you might like a lift back tomorrow.'

'I—but—I thought you were in London,' Tessa stammered.

Paul looked surprised. 'I was, for a few days,' he told her. 'Seeing an old friend from college days, back from Indonesia.'

'I see.' Tessa tried to quell the involuntary leap of relief inside her. It *hadn't* been Paul Alison had referred to in the postcard, then. 'I see—where are you staying?' she asked.

'At the local pub.'

She turned away, unable to meet the grave blue eyes any longer. 'Well, thanks for the offer, but we have our return tickets. You might as well go on.' Suddenly she spun round to face him. 'Look, Paul. My mother told me you'd been here, taking Beverley riding—talking about me behind my back. I think you owe me an explanation, don't you?' Hot colour stained her cheeks and her dark eyes flashed challengingly at him.

'There were things I wanted to ask about you,' he told her. 'So who better to talk to than your mother?'

'You've got a damned nerve!' she blazed.

'No,' he corrected. 'If I'd had the nerve I would have asked *you*! Now, thanks to your mother, I intend to. That's why I'm here.'

Tessa walked away, trying to disguise the fact that her knees were shaking. 'I haven't the slighest idea what you're . . .'

Her sentence was never finished. His hands closed on her shoulders and spun her round. She gasped with shock as his mouth came down, crushing hers into silent submission. Her first instinct was to resist, but he held her fast, pulling her rigid body relentlessly against him, sending her senses spinning till at last she relaxed in his arms—gave in to the helpless longing she had tried so hard to suppress.

His kiss was hungry and searching. It lasted a long time, and when at last he released her Tessa was too breathless to speak. Holding her face in his hands, he looked down into her eyes.

'You were saying?' he asked, his voice husky.

'Why are you here, Paul?' she whispered.

He looked at her for a long moment, then drew her towards the settee, pulling her down beside him. 'Tessa, listen. You were right—I have a lot of explaining to do, and I want you to hear me out while I still have the nerve. Until I met you I thought I knew what I wanted from life—thought I knew exactly where I was going. I was self-sufficient. Close relationships were for people who couldn't stand on their own two feet. To me, being emotionally dependent on another human being was the kind of weakness I would never allow myself to be guilty of.' He looked down at her. 'Stupidly, I thought you shared that view, so when I began to feel drawn to you I fooled myself into thinking we could work it out in a sophisticated, adult way.' He shook his head. 'I only discovered how naïve I was after the damage was done. When I woke that morning it was to a kind of revelation. I lay there realising what a complete fool I'd been. I wanted to tell you, but then I found you gone.' He ran a hand through his hair. 'You'll never know how I felt, walking from room to room and finding no trace of you—realising that I'd come to my senses too late.'

Tessa looked up at him. 'It needn't have been too late,' she told him softly.

'Ah, but you see I thought it was me who'd been caught in the trap,' Paul told her. 'How could I let you see that? How could I admit to the one weakness I'd taught myself to despise?'

She stared at him incredulously. 'Oh, Paul!'

He drew her close. 'It took Maureen, your sweet, wise

mother, to point out for me that love is no weakness but a strength—as long as we can find the courage to recognise and confess it. "Shout it to the world," was her actual advice.' He kissed her lightly on the forehead. 'So that's why I'm here—to shout it, if not to the world, then to the one person who matters. Your mother rang this morning to say you'd be alone all day. It was my last—my *only* chance.'

Tessa's eyes shone as she reached up to wind her arms around his neck, but he held her away a little.

'Wait! I haven't finished yet.' He held her face tenderly between his hands, his eyes looking deep into hers. 'I love you, Tessa,' he said quietly. 'I love you in a way that's shaken me to the very core. I can't sleep, can't eat—can't even think straight. All the corny things they put in films and books—the things I've always scoffed at—have hit me right between the eyes and completely bowled me over. You've taught me so much too, Tessa—about people as human beings and not just patients—about the enriching effect a real relationship can have, and above all, about myself.' He sighed. 'My flat is a sad empty place without you and this so-called holiday has been sheer hell because I've missed you so desperately.' He paused to kiss her softly. 'And so, my darling, the answer seems quite simple. I'd like you to marry me so that I'll never have to be without you again. I want to help you bring up Beverley and maybe later even one or two of our own.' He searched her eyes. 'If you feel the same, that is.'

For several seconds Tessa was silent, her throat too tight for words. Paul's eyes widened anxiously as he peered at her. 'Tessa? Oh God, you're not going to turn me down, are you?'

She bit her lip, laughing shakily. 'No, darling, I'm not going to turn me down.' She swallowed hard. 'I—I've got an awful lot to say on the subject, but for the moment will you please just hold me very close so that I know I'm not dreaming all this?'

When Maureen and Beverley arrived home at six o'clock that evening they found the table laid for four with the best china and glass. In the centre stood a bottle of champagne chilling in an ice bucket. Her eyes shining, Maureen took it all in and looked at her granddaughter excitedly.

'Beverley,' she whispered, 'I think there might just be a surprise for you. I think you might be going to get something you've wanted for a long time.'

Beverley ran to look out of the window. 'Granny,' she cried, standing on tiptoe to look out, 'Paul's in the garden with Mummy! And he's *kissing* her!' She looked round at her grandmother. 'Do you think that means they're going to get married?'

Maureen smiled happily to herself. 'I do believe it might,' she said, taking Beverley's hand. 'Let's go out and see what they've got to say for themselves, shall we? And keep your fingers crossed!'

THE POWER, THE PASSION, AND THE PAIN.

EMPIRE – *Elaine Bissell* _____ £2.95
Sweeping from the 1920s to modern day, this is the unforgettable
saga of Nan Mead. By building an empire of wealth and power she
had triumphed in a man's world – yet to win the man she loves,
she would sacrifice it all.

FOR RICHER OR POORER – *Ruth Alana Smith* _____ £2.50
Another compelling, witty novel by the best-selling author of
'After Midnight'. Dazzling socialite, Britt Hutton is drawn to wealthy
oil tycoon, Clay Cole. Appearances, though, are not what they seem.

SOUTHERN NIGHTS – *Barbara Kaye* _____ £2.25
A tender romance of the Deep South, spanning the wider horizons
of New York City. Shannon Parelli tragically loses her husband but
when she finds a new lover, the path of true love does not run smooth.

These three new titles will be out in bookshops from December 1988.

W⬤RLDWIDE

Available from Boots, Martins, John Menzies, WH Smith, Woolworths
and other paperback stockists.

Dare you resist...

Mills & Boon romances on cassette.

A WIDE RANGE OF TITLES AVAILABLE FROM
SELECTED BRANCHES OF WOOLWORTHS, W.H. SMITH,
BOOTS & ALL GOOD HIGH STREET STORES.

*SUGGESTED RETAIL PRICE

Doctor Nurse Romances

Romance in modern medical life

Read more about the lives and loves of doctors and nurses in the fascinatingly different backgrounds of contemporary medicine. These are the three Doctor Nurse romances to look out for next month.

FLIGHT OF SURGEONS
Barbara Perkins

A HOSPITAL CALLED JACARANTH
Jenny Ashe

NURSES IN THE HOUSE
Marion Collin

Buy them from your usual paperback stockist, or write to: Mills & Boon Reader Service, P.O. Box 236, Thornton Rd, Croydon, Surrey CR9 3RU, England. Readers in Southern Africa — write to: Independent Book Services Pty, Postbag X3010, Randburg, 2125, S. Africa.

Mills & Boon
the rose of romance

Mills & Boon

YOU'RE INVITED TO ACCEPT
4 DOCTOR NURSE ROMANCES
AND A TOTE BAG

 FREE!

Doctor Nurse

Acceptance card

| NO STAMP NEEDED | Post to: Reader Service, FREEPOST, P.O. Box 236, Croydon, Surrey. CR9 9EL |

Please note readers in Southern Africa write to:
Independant Book Services P.T.Y., Postbag X3010, Randburg 2125, S. Africa

YES! Please send me 4 free Doctor Nurse Romances and my free tote bag – and reserve a Reader Service Subscription for me. If I decide to subscribe I shall receive 6 new Doctor Nurse Romances every other month as soon as they come off the presses for £7.20 together with a FREE newsletter including information on top authors and special offers, exclusively for Reader Service subscribers. There are no postage and packing charges, and I understand I may cancel or suspend my subscription at any time. If I decide not to subscribe I shall write to you within 10 days. Even if I decide not to subscribe the 4 free novels and the tote bag are mine to keep forever. I am over 18 years of age   EP44D

NAME _____

(CAPITALS PLEASE)

ADDRESS _____

_____

_____ **POSTCODE** _____

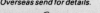

STORIES OF PASSION AND ROMANCE SPANNING FIVE CENTURIES.

CLAIM THE CROWN – *Carla Neggers* _____ £2.95
When Ashley Wakefield and her twin brother inherit a trust fund,
they are swept into a whirlwind of intrigue, suspense, danger and
romance. Past events unfold when a photograph appears of Ashley
wearing her magnificent gems.

JASMINE ON THE WIND – *Mallory Dorn Hart* _____ £3.50
The destinies of two young lovers, separated by the tides of war,
merge in this magnificent Saga of romance and high adventure set
against the backdrop of dazzling Medieval Spain.

A TIME TO LOVE – *Jocelyn Haley* _____ £2.50
Jessica Brogan's predictable, staid life is turned upside down when
she rescues a small boy from kidnappers. Should she encourage the
attentions of the child's gorgeous father, or is he simply acting
through a sense of gratitude?

These three new titles will be out in bookshops from January 1989.

W●RLDWIDE

Available from Boots, Martins, John Menzies, WH Smith, Woolworths and other
paperback stockists.